7325 6874

W9-CCC-929

Always an early riser, Brooke was up and dressed by seven.

After finding Trent's note from under her door, telling her to come to the Quinns' kitchen for breakfast, she realized she was anxious to see him again. Of course, it was only to find out if he'd heard from Rory. Maybe the family was coming home today. Maybe she'd be meeting them in a few hours.

She drove the short distance up the driveway to the house and parked her car. She hated imposing on Trent Landry again, but he was her only connection to the Quinns.

"Come in," the familiar voice called.

Once inside, she immediately smelled bacon cooking and her stomach growled in anticipation.

Standing at the stove, Trent was dressed in faded jeans and a snug black T-shirt. Oh, boy. The man was handsome, maybe not in a traditional way, but definitely in a rugged cowboy way. If you liked the cowboy type.

He tossed her a half smile. "Good morning."

Her insides fluttered. "Morning."

"Coffee's on the counter." He nodded toward the large coffeemaker.

"Oh, thank you." Maybe the caffeine would bring her to her senses.

WITHDRAWN

BEAVERTON CITY LIBRARY
BEAVERTON, OR 97005
MEMBER OF WASHINGTON COUNTY
COOPERATIVE LIBRARY SERVICES

Dear Reader,

I can't begin to tell you how excited I am about my new home with Harlequin American Romance. There's nothing I love more that writing my Western stories, and Colorado is one of my favorite places, along with Texas, Montana and Wyoming.

This new Western series, Rocky Mountain Twins, is close to my heart since twin sisters Brooke and Laurel's mother, Coralee, suffers from Alzheimer's disease.

In the first story, *Count on a Cowboy*, Brooke discovers she has a twin sister, Laurel, who's been raised by their father, Rory Quinn. Brooke goes to search for her in the small town of Hidden Springs, Colorado. Her mother's wish is to see the daughter she gave away.

When Brooke arrives at the Bucking Q Ranch, she meets handsome neighbor Trent Landry, and discovers her sister has gone to Denver. He convinces her to stay and makes her feel at home. Brooke can't help but wonder if her father and her sister will be as welcoming and include her in their family.

This story is all about finding that place to belong. I hope you enjoy it.

Patricia Thayer

WITHDRAWN

COUNT ON
A COWBOY

Patricia Thayer

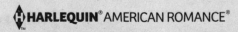

If you purchased this book without a cover you should be aware that this book is stolen property. It was reported as "unsold and destroyed" to the publisher, and neither the author nor the publisher has received any payment for this "stripped book."

Recycling programs
for this product may
not exist in your area.

ISBN-13: 978-0-373-75609-4

Count on a Cowboy

Copyright © 2016 by Patricia Wright

All rights reserved. Except for use in any review, the reproduction or utilization of this work in whole or in part in any form by any electronic, mechanical or other means, now known or hereinafter invented, including xerography, photocopying and recording, or in any information storage or retrieval system, is forbidden without the written permission of the publisher, Harlequin Enterprises Limited, 225 Duncan Mill Road, Don Mills, Ontario M3B 3K9, Canada.

This is a work of fiction. Names, characters, places and incidents are either the product of the author's imagination or are used fictitiously, and any resemblance to actual persons, living or dead, business establishments, events or locales is entirely coincidental.

This edition published by arrangement with Harlequin Books S.A.

For questions and comments about the quality of this book, please contact us at CustomerService@Harlequin.com.

® and TM are trademarks of Harlequin Enterprises Limited or its corporate affiliates. Trademarks indicated with ® are registered in the United States Patent and Trademark Office, the Canadian Intellectual Property Office and in other countries.

Printed in U.S.A.

Patricia Thayer was born and raised in Muncie, Indiana, the second in a family of eight children. She attended Ball State University before heading west, where she has called Southern California home for many years. There she's been a member of the Orange County Chapter of RWA. It's a sisterhood like no other.

When not working on a story, she might be found traveling the United States and Europe, taking in the scenery and doing story research while enjoying time with her husband, Steve. Together, they have three grown sons and four grandsons and one granddaughter, whom Patricia calls her own true-life heroes.

Books by Patricia Thayer

Harlequin Romance

Little Cowgirl Needs a Mom
The Lonesome Rancher
Tall, Dark, Texas Ranger
Once a Cowboy...
The Cowboy Comes Home
Single Dad's Holiday Wedding
Her Rocky Mountain Protector
The Cowboy She Couldn't Forget
Proposal at the Lazy S Ranch

I've been blessed with a large, wonderful family and many good friends who've stood by me and cheered me on. You've given me your love and acceptance freely, and I hope to return the favor.

And to all those families and caretakers who live with Alzheimer's disease. Bless you.

And always, Steve.

Chapter One

Brooke Harper drove along winding Interstate 70 that bordered the powerful Colorado River. It seemed as if the road was carved out of granite. Through the driver's-side window, she saw miles of lush green hillsides dotted with the rust-and-golden shades of the aspen trees that bordered the magnificent Rocky Mountains.

The scene took her breath away. Hidden Springs, Colorado, was so different from the southern Nevada landscape she'd been used to. And soon she'd be going back there. This was a short visit, so she didn't need to get used to anything. Once she was finished with her business, she'd be on her way back to Las Vegas.

Brooke slowed her seven-year-old compact, but not her heart rate, as she approached the turnoff that led to her destination. Following the GPS's directions, she took a side road, then after a few miles, another turn onto a gravel lane. She drove even slower through the grove of trees and was about to turn around when she came to a clearing, and the voice on the GPS announced, "You've reached your destination."

Just then she saw a large metal archway that read The Bucking Q Ranch.

Her heart began to race even faster. She was here. All she had to do now was put her foot on the gas pedal, drive

up to the house and ask Rory Quinn about his daughter...
Laurel Quinn.

Her sister.

Brooke felt her nerves take over and her grip tightened
on the steering wheel. After all these years being told her
father was dead...then to have her mother confess that
there was a twin sister. Or was this just one of Coralee
Harper's confused memories? Her mother had had more
of those moments the past year with the progression of
her disease.

Still riddled with guilt, Brooke knew she'd had no
choice, after her mother kept wandering off, but to put
her into a nursing home two months ago for her early-
onset Alzheimer's.

Pushing aside thoughts of Coralee, Brooke exhaled a
long breath. She wasn't here to meet her long-lost father,
only to bring back her sister, Laurel Quinn, to see their
mother. She was hoping to find out if Coralee's ramblings
were true.

She continued down the wide gravel road lined with
pine and aspen trees that opened into a clearing where
several large structures came into view: a glossy white
barn and five outbuildings. A long split-rail fence ran beside a pasture housing several beautiful horses. The fence
also lined the yard around a magnificent stone-and-cedar
two-story house.

Brooke parked the car and climbed out, waiting for
someone to come out, but the place looked deserted. She
started up the lengthy drive and noticed decorative ribbons draped over the fence, each post tied with flowers.
She reached the house where baskets of flowers lined the
large porch.

She knew she could be interrupting something, but that
didn't stop her. She went around the house to the back

and froze, seeing rows of white chairs with a white runner down the middle, leading to a floral archway. On one of the chairs, she found a program detailing for Laurel Quinn and Jack Aldrich's nuptials. Great. She was crashing her sister's wedding.

TRENT LANDRY RACED his truck to the Bucking Q. A lot of good it had done him to go chasing into town after Aldrich. The creep was long gone, and so was their money. He took the corner off the highway too fast and kicked gravel up behind him, but he didn't slow down. He needed to stop Rory and Laurel from going after the runaway groom.

"Dammit!" Trent's fist hit the wheel. He knew that something wasn't right about the guy. "I should have listened to my gut." A dozen years in Special Forces and he'd let a two-bit hustler run off with their money.

His cell phone rang and he pushed the button on the wheel to answer Rory's call. "Rory, what's going on?"

"We're on our way to Denver. Laurel's hell-bent on finding Jack so he can explain his disappearance. I could barely talk her into letting us go along."

He was afraid of this. "Not a good idea, Rory. Aldrich has already broken the law. He's not going to let anyone take him into custody."

"I know," Rory said, his voice an angry whisper. "But I'm the one who hired this jerk. I gave him access to my daughter. Hell, he asked me for her hand in marriage. Dammit, I need to protect Laurel now."

Trent ran his hand over his jaw. "Okay, but you better be back in forty-eight hours, or I'm coming for you."

"Deal." There was a long pause. "I'm sorry about this mess, Trent, and what it's done to our partnership. I hate to ask any more, but could you let the wedding guests know…?"

"Sure, I can handle it. We'll talk later."

Trent disconnected the call.

He would do anything to protect the Quinns. Years ago, his father, Wade Landry, and Rory Quinn had ridden the rodeo circuit together. After the two retired, they settled here to raise their families and cattle. Then suddenly one day their tranquility had ended, and it had all gone bad for the Landrys…

Trent quickly shook away the dark memories. He had to deal with today. He pulled up to the Quinns' home and saw the car with Nevada plates. Who was the out-of-state guest?

"Time to find out."

Placing his Stetson on his head, he climbed out and glanced toward the deserted barn. The men had left early to repair a stretch of downed fence, so they could get back in time to get cleaned up for the wedding. Trent thought to his own rented tux, hanging in the back of his truck. Now he had to tell everyone the ceremony wasn't going to happen.

Trent cursed and started off around the back of the house. He was immediately greeted by rows of empty white chairs. A long white runner spanned the middle aisle, dotted with rose petals, and ending at a huge flower-covered archway where the bride and groom were to exchange vows. The real star of the show was the incredible view of the north-facing mountain range sprinkled with the fiery colors of the aspen's fall leaves mixed with evergreen ponderosa pines. A perfect setting for a late afternoon wedding. That was if you were into believing in happily-ever-after.

Feeling the warm late September sun, Trent rolled his

sleeves on his Western shirt. Time to get to work. He paused when something caught his eye. A woman walking toward him.

Great, an early wedding guest. He took a second glance and something looked familiar about her. She came up the aisle in long easy strides. Dark trousers covered her long slender legs and a cream-colored silky blouse showed off gentle curves. Her chin-length hair was a silky, golden blond with some rich highlights. When she reached him a tentative smile turned up the corners of her full mouth, causing more of a reaction than he wanted to admit.

He swallowed and asked, "May I help you with something?"

"I hope so. I'm looking for Laurel Quinn," she said.

"Well, you just missed her. She's not here."

Brooke tried not to react to the man's abruptness. She considered going into town and returning another day. Too late. She straightened her shoulders. "Then could you tell me where I can find Rory Quinn?"

He folded his large arms over his wide chest, and he spread his stance as if to look intimidating. It was working.

"And who are you?"

She refused to back away, not after it had taken her so long to get here. "Brooke Harper." She arched an eyebrow. "Are you related to the Quinns?"

He shook his head. "I'm Trent Landry, a family friend and business partner. And again, why do you want to see Rory?"

She glanced away from the man's dark gaze. She'd dealt with a lot of businessmen in her job, but this guy was good at intimidation. Either he was military or law enforcement. But she could handle it. "I believe that is between Mr. Quinn and myself."

"Well, you can believe whatever you want, but both Rory and Laurel Quinn will be away for a few days. So why don't you return then?" He tried to read her eyes. "Or you can tell me what this is about and when I talk with Rory, I can relay your message."

Brooke didn't have a lot of time or choices. So she'd either wait until the Quinns returned home, or she'd have to take more time off work. But how much did she want to tell this man? Definitely nothing about her connection to Rory Quinn.

"Laurel Quinn is my…half sister."

How can Laurel have a sister?

"Is that so?"

Trent watched Brooke Harper's hands shake, but she managed to extract papers from her oversize purse and give them to him.

His gaze didn't waver from those intriguing green eyes until he opened the folded sheets, then finally glanced over a birth certificate, stating that Coralee Harper gave birth to a female child on the twelfth day of December, 1988.

Trent looked at the other paper, a custody agreement, giving Rory Quinn full custody of his daughter Laurel Kathryn Harper. These weren't the originals, but he couldn't discount them, either. If true, that meant Diane Quinn wasn't Laurel's biological mother?

Damn, this was above his pay grade.

He studied the pretty blonde, looking for a resemblance. Her large eyes were deep green in color, her fair skin was flawless and her full mouth… He halted the survey, realizing he needed to stop getting distracted by her. Brooke Harper's news could destroy the Quinn family.

He needed to get ahold of Rory. "Excuse me. I need

to make a call." He [...]
in the familiar number[...]
had been constructed in the [...]
guests for the Quinn-Aldrich w[...]

Then came sunrise and there was [...]
When Laurel couldn't get ahold of Jack [...]
had gone out to the general contractor's tem[...]
dence, the small trailer at the building site. He'd [...]
completely empty. Obviously, Jack had cleared out so[...]
time during the night.

Now, four hours before the ceremony the groom had disappeared; also all their money for the construction of the cabins was gone with him. If that wasn't enough, this woman had shown up and claimed to be Laurel's sister.

Rory's phone rang and rang, and finally went to voice mail. "Please leave a message..."

"Rory, this is Trent." He rubbed the back of his neck. "I need you to call me, right away. Something has come up here, and no, it's nothing to do with finding Aldrich."

Just as Trent disconnected the call, he turned to see a truck, painted with the sign All Occasions Catering on its side, pull into the drive. Great, something else he had to deal with. And the troubles didn't stop, he thought, remembering the fifty-plus wedding guests arriving soon.

Around the barn appeared the ranch truck, and four ranch hands piled out. He needed help. Trent punched the ranch foreman's phone number.

"Hey, Trent what's up?" Chet answered.

"Hi, Chet. Has Rory called you today?"

"No, he hasn't. Why?"

"There's been a change of plans. Wedding's been called off."

"What?"

Trent didn't want to go into details now. "Yeah, and

handle
...t to the
...that the
...ey thank

...any more,"

soon as they get

...es the help."

Do you need any-

thing else

"Yeah, a few ... the chairs and tables
back to the rental place

"Sure. Let me get the flatbed and we'll be up in a few."

"Thanks, Chet."

Trent hung up and quickly went to handle his next prob-
lem, the caterer. Even bigger trouble was when he found
Miss Harper talking to the man in the white uniform.
He headed over to find out what she was saying to him.

Trent knew the catering owner, Bill Cummings, from
town. "Hey, Bill." Trent shook the older man's hand.

"Hi, Trent." Bill grinned. "I hear from lovely Miss
Harper here that there's been a change of plans."

Just what had she told him? He sent her a glaring look,
and got a sweet smile in return. Feeling a sudden jolt of
awareness, he turned back to Bill. "Yes, the wedding has
been called off."

"I'm sorry to hear that." Bill frowned. "But there's no
refunds, I told that to Rory when he paid the deposit."

"I'm sure they understood that when they hired you."
He silently cursed Aldrich again for causing all this trouble. Not that he cared, but this news would be all over

town once Bill's wife, Bess, learned of the cancellation. Nothing he could do about that.

Bill looked sympathetic about the situation. "So what do you want me to do with all this food?" He motioned to the truck.

"Donate it." Brooke Harper stepped forward.

"I worked for a large hotel and when we have left-over food from our events, we take it to a shelter or soup kitchen."

"Do I take it all? And what about the cake? It's three tiers with the bride and groom…"

"Donate everything." Trent didn't have time or energy to think of a place. "Bill, you decide where it goes."

He glanced toward the barn to see Larry and Ollie getting into the truck and heading out to the gate to greet the guests and send them home.

Bill snapped his fingers. "St. Theresa's Catholic Church has a shelter." He looked at Trent as he pulled out his phone. "Do you think that will be all right with Rory and Diane? I mean, I know they go to the Methodist Church on Grant Street."

"I think when it's a charitable act, it doesn't matter," Trent told him. "And since Rory instructed me to handle things, I vote for St. Theresa's. I really appreciate you doing this for the family."

With a nod, Bill walked back to the truck, holding the phone against his ear.

Trent took Miss Harper by the arm and guided her aside. "I wasn't able to get ahold of Rory yet, but I left a message for him to call me back. Why don't you give me your cell number and I'll call you when I hear from him?"

She hesitated, her gaze searching his. "I think I'll hang around for a little while…just in case he calls…soon. Besides, it looks like you could use some help here."

Before Trent could argue the point, she walked toward the men and began directing them to specific jobs: folding and stacking the tables and chairs, then loading them on the truck. Since he didn't want to deal with more questions, he didn't stop her.

Over the next hour, the crew of men managed to get everything loaded onto the flatbed. Chet jumped behind the wheel and drove off toward town and the rental company.

That was fairly easy. Trent grabbed a bottle of water that had been retrieved from the kitchen and took a long drink. He looked around and found Brooke Harper standing at the floral archway. He grabbed another bottle. Determined to tell her it was time to leave, he walked to her, but paused, catching her biting her full lower lip, a frown creasing her high forehead.

She seemed to have sensed his presence, turning with a smile. "This is so beautiful. It's a shame to waste all these lovely flowers."

He handed her the cold water bottle. "What do you suggest we do with them—ship them off to a hospital?

"They'd probably appreciate them."

She took a drink and Trent watched her slender neck bend back, exposing the smooth skin.

He quickly turned away to the white arch intertwined with greenery and colorful flowers. He inhaled the soft scent and didn't know if it was the blooms or the woman. "Okay, I'll have one of the men take care of the delivery. I don't want Laurel to have any reminders of today."

Brooke turned her head. Her green eyes flashed him a look that reminded him a lot of Laurel. "I'm sorry. She must be devastated."

Trent shrugged. "Probably, but I didn't get a chance to talk to her. She took off to Denver to find him. Her parents went with her. That's why Rory isn't here."

"Then I showed up and added to your troubles."

He didn't disagree. "This isn't the best time to announce to Laurel that she has a sister and a biological mother—who gave her up."

BROOKE WORKED HARD not to look away from Trent Landry. His cowboy hat might have shaded his eyes, but she felt the heat from the rich coffee color. He seemed to be able to reach deep inside her and pull out more than she wanted him to know. But her news wasn't for him, it was for Rory and Laurel.

"And that's why Coralee wants to see her. To explain why she had to give her up."

The tall, muscular man's dark gaze sent her a glaring look. "By signing away her rights, she made a promise not to contact Laurel." He folded his arms over his chest. "That's what full custody means. And now she's breaking it, by pushing herself into her daughter's life."

"She has a good reason."

"What, guilt, because she gave her away?"

Brooke had trouble staying calm, but she knew she had to focus on her mother's wish. "I'm sure that Rory will understand why Coralee wants to see Laurel this one time."

He frowned. "Why, is she dying?"

Brooke's chest tightened with emotion. "Something like that. Coralee has early-onset Alzheimer's."

Chapter Two

"Look, Mr. Landry," Brooke began, still having trouble reading the man. "I didn't come here to argue with you. I made a promise to my mother."

"It's Trent," he insisted.

She nodded, trying to rein in her frustration. "Trent. Please call me Brooke."

He smiled and she quickly lost her train of thought.

"Okay, Brooke. Why don't we go inside and sit down? I think we've earned a break."

Brooke let him escort her up the back steps and through a large mudroom that had a front-loading washer and dryer. On the other wall was a long row of hooks that held a collection of cowboy hats. That was where Trent placed his hat, then motioned her into the next space.

She paused in the doorway and her gaze searched the farm-style kitchen, including a brick fireplace. Lining the walls were white cabinets with black metal hinges and knobs decorating the fronts. Dark-stained butcher-block counters held small appliances, but left plenty of room for making meals or baking cookies. Oh, my, the room was as big as her entire apartment.

Suddenly she was second-guessing her decision to come here. But for months, Coralee had begged her, cried about her other daughter, Laurel. The baby she gave away.

What if Rory Quinn didn't care and he threw her off the property?

Brooke stiffened, feeling Trent's hand against her spine.

"Let's sit over here."

He directed her to an oval table in front of a picture window overlooking the pasture of grazing cattle.

She just realized she didn't know much about this family. Only what was on the website for Bucking Q Cattle Company. "How many Quinns live here?"

"There's just the three of them. Rory, Diane, his wife, and the one daughter, Laurel."

Just one daughter that he knows about, she thought, looking out at the incredible mountains through the glass. "It must have been fun to grow up on a ranch." She turned around to see Trent's curious look.

"Yeah, it is, but there's a lot of work, too." He went to the refrigerator and took out a pitcher of iced tea. "Looks like Bill left some food here, too."

Brooke wasn't surprised. "I hope you don't mind, but I also asked him to leave some of the food in the bunkhouse for the men."

He stopped pouring the tea and stared at her.

Was he upset?

"I mean, they've worked hard today. It's nice that they can have a good meal tonight. Chet talked very highly of Laurel."

"They all think highly of Laurel, and yeah, the men were all invited to the wedding."

"That's nice."

"You won't find nicer people than Rory and Diane."

She hoped she got a chance to find that out. "You've known them for a long time."

He nodded. "Years ago, my dad, Wade, and Rory rode

the rodeo circuit together. Then when they retired, Rory bought the Bucking Q and Dad came a few years later and bought the ranch next door, the Lucky Bar L. So you can say Rory's known me since I was born."

"If they'd been friends all these years, I bet your dad would know about Coralee."

A distant look appeared on Trent's face. "He might, but he died almost two years ago."

"I'm sorry," she said, hating that she was bringing up sad memories.

He nodded. "So am I. Since I'm only four years older than Laurel, I can't remember something like that. When my folks settled here, Rory was married and had baby Laurel."

"I guess I'm just going to have to get answers from Mr. Quinn."

Trent brought the glasses to the table, then turned the chair around and straddled it. He took a long drink. "I never asked where you're from."

"Nevada. Las Vegas."

"Are you older or younger than Laurel?"

Brooke froze a second. "Younger." That wasn't a lie.

He studied her closely, then asked, "What do you do in Las Vegas?"

"Right now, I'm a card dealer, but I just graduated college and I'm hoping to hear soon about a hotel-management position. That's the reason I can't stay long. It a great opportunity, especially with the added expense of my mother's long-term care…"

Trent arched an eyebrow. "Are you thinking about asking for help from the Quinns?"

She reared back. "Of course not. Believe me, Mr. Landry, I know very well that Rory Quinn doesn't owe my mother a thing."

She started to stand, but Trent placed his hand on her arm to prevent her leaving.

"I apologize," he said. "I'm protective of my friends, and today had to be the worst day to show up here."

"I don't doubt that, and I'm sorry for all your troubles. But I'm here now," she countered. "And if Mr. Quinn calls you, you can let him handle it."

"It's Rory. Everyone calls him Rory."

An ache touched deep in her chest. She would have liked to call the man Dad, but her mother had taken that choice away from both of them.

TWO HOURS LATER, Trent had finished canceling the rest of the wedding services, wishing he could cancel all the curious phone calls from guests, too. He finally turned off the ringer on the house phone, but watched to see if Rory called. Everything else he let go to the answering machine.

When Brooke went into the bathroom, Trent punched in Rory's number again. He listened to the ringing until it went to voice mail.

"Rory, it's Trent again. Please call me as soon as you can." He ended the call as Brooke walked back into the kitchen.

"Did you call Rory again?"

"Yeah, but he's still not answering," he told her.

"Are you worried about him?"

Trent shook his head, but he was concerned. What if they'd found Aldrich? The man on the run could be dangerous. "Not the way you think. Rory's easygoing, but Laurel can get pretty hot when she's crossed. I wouldn't want to be Jack Aldrich if she catches up to him. Which I hope she doesn't since he's broken the law and might not care how he gets away."

"Broke the law?"

"Jack didn't just run out on his wedding, he stole from us. He cleared all the money out of our escrow account."

She gasped. "Oh, no. He worked for you?"

"The man was the general contractor hired to build several rental cabins for us. Laurel got involved with him. Jack fed her a bunch of romantic rubbish and the next thing we knew, the whirlwind romance turned into a quick wedding—" he checked his watch "—that should have taken place about an hour ago. The one good thing is that the wedding didn't happen."

Trent stood and walked to the window. He'd already said more than he intended, but soon the news would be all over town. He sighed and looked out, seeing the last of the sun going behind the mountains. Time was running out on what to do about Brooke Harper.

He turned around and she looked up at him with those wide eyes, as if she expected him to tell her something bad.

"Where are you staying in town?"

She looked up at him. "I don't have a place yet. I drove straight here. Can you recommend a hotel?"

He'd seen her old car and knew she probably didn't have much money to waste. Even knowing Brooke's news could change the Quinn family forever he couldn't send her away. Besides, he wanted her to stay close, especially because of the possibility she was Laurel's sister.

"I know of a place," he said. "That is, if you don't mind the sparse furnishings."

She wrinkled that cute nose. "How sparse?"

"Oh, the place has a nice bed and a table and chairs, but no cable or HBO."

"I can afford a little more than basic."

"But they're ten miles away in town. I can promise you

this place is clean—in fact, it's brand-new. We just finished our first hunting cabin. I can get you some towels and sheets and a coffeepot, but that's about all."

"You mean stay here at the ranch?"

With his nod, she hesitated. "How do you think the Quinns will feel about that?"

"If you've been honest about why you're here, there shouldn't be any problem."

A sudden look came over her face and he caught a slight resemblance to Laurel. Or had he just talked himself into seeing something?

"As long as it has electricity, the place sounds perfect to me," she told him. "How much?"

"No charge for the first night. Then when Rory gets back, hopefully tomorrow, he'll make a decision about lengthening your visit."

Brooke's gaze darted from his. "I'm not planning on staying that long. I only wanted to see Laurel."

"I'd rather you talk with Rory first, especially since as far as I know, Laurel hasn't been told anything."

"All right, I promise not to say anything until I talk to Rory." She smiled. "And thank you for letting me stay here."

He sighed. "Now that's settled, let's eat some of the wedding supper. Seems someone should enjoy it."

He went to the refrigerator and took out containers of chicken breasts and scalloped potatoes. There were rolls and sides of green beans and asparagus.

He was suddenly hungry, realizing he hadn't eaten since breakfast. What about Brooke? When was her last meal? His gaze scanned her slender frame. She'd worked hard, too.

Yet, he got the feeling she was leaving a lot out of the story about Coralee. Or was it her nervousness from finally meeting her half sister? And if true, how would Laurel take this? She and Diane had always been close. Would this news change that?

He knew his way around the Quinns' kitchen, having grown up here over the years The place had been like a second home for him and his brother, Chris. So much had changed since those days. His brother was gone, his parents had divorced and his father had passed away. And he'd finally come back home to exorcise the ghosts. That was still a work in progress.

He took down two plates from the cupboard and filled them with food, then put one in the microwave. Ten minutes later he was seated across from Brooke.

"This is delicious," she told him.

"I agree. Bill and Bess are the best cooks in town. They also own a diner, the B&B Café, off Main Street. If you're around long enough, you should stop by."

He cut his chicken and ate a piece. "It's just down-home cooking, but good. I've eaten enough MREs over the years to appreciate the real stuff."

She stopped eating. "You were in the military?"

Nodding, he swallowed. "Over a dozen years in the army, Special Forces."

"Were you deployed?"

A sudden sadness came over him as memories flashed in his head. "Three times. When my father passed away, I decided it was time to opt out so I came back and took over running the ranch." He owed Wade Landry that much.

He looked at her to discover her watching him. Those emerald eyes were dark with emotion. "I'm glad you made it back home." She swallowed and said in a raspy whisper, "Thank you for your service."

When he'd been in uniform, he'd heard the words many

times, but he felt her sincerity. He nodded, then looked down at his plate. His food was cold, and so was his appetite. "I guess I'm not as hungry as I thought."

She fought a yawn. "You piled a lot of food on our plates. Maybe I can save mine for later. Is there a microwave in the cabin?"

"Yeah. I'll wrap it up for you to take it." He stood and picked up her plate, found the foil and busied himself putting her food together.

This woman was getting to him, and that couldn't happen. He didn't know her at all, and that meant she was off-limits.

So keep your hormones in check. Your first and only job is to protect the Quinns.

From his experience, trouble came in all kinds of packages, especially tall, slender blondes with big emerald-green eyes that could turn a man inside out.

He glanced over his shoulder. Not going to happen.

THIRTY MINUTES LATER, Trent pulled his truck in front of the recently completed log cabin. He climbed out and turned on a flashlight to find his way to the front door. He inhaled the scent of fresh-cut wood.

Maybe bringing Brooke here was a bad idea. She would be out here all by herself. Not that he should have to worry about her, but he did. After unlocking the door, he swung it open, reached inside for the switch and flipped on the lights. The small porch was illuminated and he waited for Brooke as she parked her compact next to his vehicle. She got out and reached into the backseat for a duffel bag, then walked to him.

"This is nice," she remarked looking around.

"I know it still looks like a construction site, but in a few months with all the trees around it will be peaceful."

"And isolated." Just then off in the distance a coyote howled. She tensed.

"You're used to a city that never sleeps, so of course this seems cut off from everything, but really it's not that far from the ranch house. By road it takes longer." He pointed over the rise. "In the morning if you head that way over the rise, you'll see the house about a hundred and fifty yards away."

"Okay."

Taking the bag from her, he pushed open the door to show her the three-room cabin. He turned on another light in the small kitchen that overlooked the living space. There was a dark leather sofa pushed up against the wall, a table and two chairs on the other side. A large area rug covered the floors.

"This is lovely," she said as she headed to the doorway that led to a bedroom that had a queen bed and a set of bunk beds against the other wall. Then she looked into the bath with a spacious tiled shower stall, a long counter with double sinks and a toilet.

"You say this is a hunting cabin?"

"Hunting and fishing." He nodded behind him. "We've also started construction on a large building for meetings, and social gatherings."

"Oh, that will be nice." She smiled. "It's surprising what people will pay to get away from life's distractions."

"You should know all about that, working in Las Vegas."

She walked out to the common area. "Yes, during college I interned with a hotel that had me train with the concierge that booked special packages for corporations."

"Sounds like you enjoy your work."

She nodded. "Yes, I do. My degree is in hotel management."

"My partnership with the Quinns is a small operation, and that's how we want it. Less stress. Now that's exactly what we have right now. Stress." He shook his head. "Shows you can't trust everyone. If you need anything, just call my cell." They copied each other's numbers. "Guess that's it. I'll be staying in the cabin next door so I can be here quickly. Good night."

He walked out, climbed in his truck and drove off. Then she saw him stop just a few yards down the road. A few seconds later a light went on and she could see the outline of the cabin. Okay, she wasn't alone. A warm feeling spread through her: she wasn't used to being watched over.

Two HOURS LATER, Brooke tugged at the multicolored quilt over her and leaned back against the queen-size bed's carved headboard.

The silence was deafening. Not even a television for white noise, or a computer to get up and Google something.

She sat up. What was she doing here? She had a great opportunity for a job at a large chain hotel. She needed to be in Las Vegas. She couldn't let this opportunity slip through her fingers. Not when she could get a better paying job to help with her mother. So much of Coralee's special care wasn't covered by her insurance.

The heck with it. Brooke finally got out of bed, but wrapped the quilt around her pajama-clad body to ward off the chill. She walked into the main room and turned on the wall heater, then sat down on the sofa. Only a soft light from the kitchen area illuminated the space.

She released a long breath, and looked around. This place was so different from her one-bedroom apartment in the shoddy part of town. Once she got her new job, she hoped she could afford to move. And if she could get her mother on better insurance that would help with some of the extra expenses.

Over her lifetime, Brooke had accepted Coralee's faults and weaknesses—men being at the top of the list. So why would she walk away from a man like rodeo star Rory Quinn? Maybe he didn't want Coralee. At the very least, wouldn't he have paid child support for his children? And why did her mother tell Rory about only one baby?

Tears welled in her eyes as Brooke thought back to the years of struggle while Coralee tried to make it as a singer. She could even remember all her mother's promises.

"All I need, sweetie, is that one big break, then we'll have a nice home, and you can have all the toys and party dresses a little girl could want."

There was never a big break, only more jobs in sleazy clubs, more drinking and men moving into their apartment to cover Coralee's disappointment. Brooke shivered. Some of the men were frightening and others were abusive. And then there were the ones who'd stolen everything from them.

Years of overindulgence with alcohol and cigarettes, until Coralee's voice and looks were gone. She could only find work as a waitress in a diner.

That job had ended last year when her fifty-two-year-old mother was diagnosed with early-onset Alzheimer's. Then six months ago in January, Brooke found she couldn't leave her alone any longer. Not when she began to wander off from the apartment, left water running in the bathtub, and took things from the store without paying.

She had no choice but to move Coralee into assisted-care living. She found a small group home that would take Alzheimer's patients. Brooke was also lucky that she could work there to offset some of the cost of the care.

Brooke wiped the tears from her cheeks. She didn't

have the money for live-in help. The only chance she had to make their lives better had been to finish college. Even with the possibility of her new job, it was still going to be rough going.

So the trip here had taken a lot of her meager savings, and every minute Brooke stayed in Colorado meant she wasn't working. The family living here didn't have that problem. Laurel Quinn had no idea what it was like to be Coralee's daughter.

Chapter Three

At 4:00 a.m. the next morning, Trent swung his legs over the side of the single cot. He'd gotten soft the past two years. In the army, he'd been able to sleep anywhere. Now, sleep eluded him.

Rubbing a hand over his face, he stood and walked to the window. He might as well get up.

The night was cool, but he welcomed the chill against his skin. A certain blonde had caused him more than an inconvenience since her arrival not even twenty-four hours ago.

Brooke Harper made a man take notice, and he noticed all right. Enough that he'd tossed and turned most of the night. She had him trying to recall how long it had been since he'd spent time with a woman, a woman to share a long night with.

He released a long breath, trying to ease the tension in his body. Not that he'd do anything about it with Brooke. She had a connection to Laurel, and there was a strong possibility that they were sisters. Besides, Brooke Harper was the kind who needed a steady guy, who gave her promises—a home and kids.

Sadness washed over him. He'd never be that guy. He was better off alone. Dreams of family had disappeared long ago.

He shook off the memories, and looked out the window. The sky was still dark, but the moon was still aglow and he could see the occupied cabin about fifty yards away. He could also see a light on.

Couldn't Brooke sleep, either, or was she afraid? His protective instincts kicked in. They were in an isolated area and she didn't know him from Adam.

He shook his head, thinking about the crazy events of the day: the groom running off, a canceled wedding, then a long-lost sister showing up. And Brooke Harper was determined to meet her sister. Why, after all these years, hadn't Rory and Diane told Laurel the truth about her birth?

So many questions that needed answers. Something told him that the pretty Miss Harper knew more than she was saying. "You need to call me, Rory. I can't do anything until you give me some answers. If not for me, then to Laurel."

Trent walked to the lone chair in the room, grabbed his jeans and pulled them on. Since he was wide awake, he might as well get some work done. Back at his place he could feed the stock. Not that he didn't have capable men to do chores; he just needed to burn off this energy. He put on his shirt and buttoned it, then pulled on boots. He grabbed his hat off the table and headed toward the door.

Once he finished his work, he'd come back in time to make breakfast for Brooke and maybe learn some more about their pretty visitor. And with any luck Rory would call him.

ALWAYS AN EARLY RISER, Brooke was up and dressed by 7:00 a.m. in a pair of jeans, a white blouse and a navy pullover sweater. After finding Trent's note from under her door, telling her to come to the Quinns' kitchen for breakfast, she realized she was anxious to see him again. Of course, it was only to find out if he'd heard from Rory. Maybe the family was coming home today. Maybe she'd be meeting them in a few hours.

Right now, she would do anything for a cup of coffee. She drove the short distance up the driveway to the house and parked her car. She got out, walked up and knocked on the back door. She hated imposing on Trent Landry again, but he was her only connection to the Quinns.

"Come in," the familiar voice called.

Once inside, she immediately smelled bacon cooking and her stomach growled in anticipation.

Standing at the stove, Trent was dressed in faded jeans and a fitted Western shirt. Oh, boy. The man was handsome, maybe not in a traditional way, but definitely in a rugged-cowboy way. If you liked the cowboy type.

He tossed her a half smile. "Good morning."

Her insides fluttered. "Morning."

"Coffee's on the counter." He nodded toward the large coffeemaker.

She walked over. "Thank you." Maybe the caffeine-laced drink would bring her to her senses.

"What's your pleasure?" He pointed to the open carton of eggs. "Scrambled, sunny-side up or over easy?"

She filled the mug. "Don't feel you need to feed me."

"I'm eating, so you might as well. It could be a long day…waiting for that phone call. After seeing you in action yesterday, I might decide to put you to work."

She cupped the mug in her hands and inhaled the wonderful aroma. "Okay, I'll have scrambled, but only one."

"Good choice. Will you put some bread in the toaster?"

"Of course." She took a sip, then reached for the loaf of whole wheat on the counter and put in four slices. Then she picked up her mug again and took a sip. "Oh, this tastes so good," she purred.

Trent looked at her, his eyes narrowed. "Good coffee is important."

"I agree, and I probably drink far too much. Between work and school, I needed the extra boost."

She leaned against the counter and watched the large man's fluid movements as he worked at his tasks. Her gaze went to the worn denim that molded his delicious backside and muscular thighs. A shot of awareness hit her like the caffeine she was drinking. Her attention moved up to his clean-shaven face and strong jaw. His dark hair was trimmed short around the ears and slightly wavy on top.

He glanced at her. "So you're one of those who hang out in those specialty coffee places."

She shook her head. "I wish, but my budget can't afford their prices. I make my own coffee at home, or at work."

He gave her another odd look.

"What's the matter? Did I say something wrong?"

"No, just hoping your new job pays enough for you to splurge on an occasional fancy mocha latte."

She went on to explain. "The job isn't a sure thing yet. I'm one of four people they're looking at, but I interned for them last year, and I'm hoping that works in my favor."

He poured the egg mixture into the sizzling skillet. "What's the job?"

"The position is for second-shift front desk manager."

The toast popped up. "Eventually, I want to get into sales and marketing. The Dream Chaser Hotel chain is a good place to get experience."

Trent dished out the cooked eggs and brought them to the table, then filled two glasses of orange juice while Brooke buttered the toast and stacked the slices on a plate.

He waited until she took a seat then sat down across

from her. Not used to eating with someone, let alone a man who showed such manners, she decided she liked it.

Nibbling on a piece of toast, Brooke sat back as Trent dug eagerly into his pile of eggs.

He motioned to her food. "My dad used to say you'll never grow if you don't eat."

"Seems you took him up on that," she said without thinking. "I...just meant you're a large man."

TRENT MANAGED TO choke down his food as Brooke's wide-eyed gaze assessed him. Damn, if he didn't feel the heat rising between them. He swallowed again. "You need muscle for ranching."

Brooke's gaze moved to his chest. "I can see how that would help."

The warmth spread to his groin. "For a lot of years the army kept me on a strict workout regimen. Old habits die hard."

"So you lift weights."

"Mainly I lift hay bales and wrestle a few steers."

"You really do all that work?"

Was Brooke that innocent, or was she playing a game? Either way, she was making it impossible to concentrate... on his meal. "You do if you want to run a successful operation."

She took a bite of eggs, and his attention went to her mouth. "I thought you were renting out fishing and hunting cabins."

He picked up a strip of bacon and ate half in one bite. "You can do both. Rory and I raise cattle first, a mama-and-calf operation, but it's a good idea to have another source of income, especially during the lean years. Besides, I like to hunt and fish."

"Is this a lean year?"

"It's not too bad. There's been enough water and grass for the herd. Why are you so interested?"

With her fair skin he could easily see her blush. "Just curious about my sister growing up here." She shrugged. "And I've lived in Las Vegas all my life. The desert is beautiful, but so different from Colorado."

"I'm not a fan of the desert. Over the years, I saw far too much of it." He fought to keep those memories at bay. He pointed to the window. "I prefer the Rocky Mountains in my backyard."

"So you were born and raised here?"

More questions, he thought. "Until I was fourteen when my parents divorced. I moved to Denver with my mom."

"I'm sorry." She offered him a hesitant smile. "At least you got to come back to live here."

For far too many years he'd lost touch with his dad. He'd regret that forever and that he'd never gotten to see his little brother grow up… "Yeah, I got to come back here."

Before Brooke could speak again, his cell phone rang. Trent took it out of his pocket. "It's Rory. I'll be right back." He got up from the table as he pressed the talk button and walked out to the mudroom. He needed privacy for what he had to say.

"Rory. What the hell is going on?" he asked.

"Good morning to you, too," the older man answered.

Trent ran his fingers through his hair. "Sorry, I've been worried. Another hour and I'd be in my truck and headed for Denver. Is everyone okay?"

"Yes, we're fine. And no, we haven't found Jack. Every place that Laurel knew about turned out to be a dead end."

"How about letting your friends know you're all right?"

"I was hoping to have some news to tell you before I called, but no such luck."

Trent turned around to see Brooke watching him from the other room. "How about that I have some important news for you."

"Has that creep come back to Hidden Springs?"

"No, Aldrich hasn't shown up. That would be too easy for us."

"Yeah, and if you'd gotten ahold of him…all that would be left would be to dispose of the body." A laugh came over the line. "I know you Special Forces types. Get in and get out before anyone knows what happened."

"Believe me, I wish I had a chance with this guy, but that's not what I wanted to talk to you about."

Trent paused, trying to figure out how to phrase his words. "This is a different matter altogether."

There was a pause, then Rory said, "Just tell me straight out, son."

"You had a visitor show up yesterday right after you left. A woman named Brooke Harper. She says she's Laurel's half sister."

"The hell you say?"

"Strange, but true. Rory, have you ever known a woman by the name of Coralee Harper?"

There was more silence, then Rory finally spoke. "Coralee Harper came to the ranch?"

"No, but her daughter, Brooke Harper, arrived yesterday just hours after you all left."

Rory cursed.

"So Laurel's adopted?" Trent already knew the answer, but needed Rory to confirm it.

"Since I'm Laurel's biological father there was no adoption, I got full custody. It cost me enough money to get Coralee to sign my daughter over to me. And she was never supposed to contact me or Laurel again."

"Well, Coralee's other daughter is sitting in your kitchen, waiting to see Laurel."

"Get her the hell out of there."

"Hear me out first, Rory," he said, wondering why he was playing Miss Harper's advocate. Yet, he found himself calming Rory down and telling him the story about Coralee's Alzheimer's and her wanting to see Laurel one last time.

"No way. That woman has caused me enough problems. I'm not sure I even believe this story. It's more than likely Coralee just wants more money."

"That's why you need to tell Laurel, and let her decide if she wants to come home and meet her sister."

He heard the long sigh, then the curse. "We always meant to tell Laurel, but we kept putting it off. Damn, I knew this would happen…" Rory's voice wandered off.

"Well, it looks like you don't have a choice now."

"Okay, then you tell me just how in the hell do I do it?"

"Like you always tell me, straight-out."

"I guess you're right." Rory released a long breath. "I need to ask you another favor. Trent, could you have that friend of yours, the PI, investigate Coralee? And have him look into Aldrich, too. The police here haven't been able to help us."

"Consider it done. I'll contact Cody Marsh today. So when should I expect you back here?"

"Give us a few days," Rory said. "You're right, Diane and I need to explain all this to Laurel. This news—and she's still dealing with the aftershocks of Aldrich's betrayal—is going to take some time."

"So you want me to send Brooke back to Las Vegas?"

"No, I don't want her to leave until you find out the truth. Do you think you can keep her there a little while longer? If Coralee is running a scam, I swear… Just keep her there."

"I'll do my best. But please, Rory, just get back here soon."

After promising to stay in touch by phone, Trent hung up and walked back into the kitchen. He wasn't about to apologize for wanting privacy. "Rory asks if you'll stay a few days until he gets back. So how about I show you around the ranch?"

BROOKE DIDN'T LIKE how Trent just brushed over the important parts of the phone call. "Wait a minute. What did Rory ask? Does he remember Coralee? Is he going to tell Laurel about being her daughter?"

Trent held up a hand. "Slow down. First of all, yes, he remembers Coralee. And that's all I'm saying because this is his story to tell you."

She wasn't happy. "So I'm just supposed to sit around and wait until Rory Quinn decides to come home."

"No. You can return to Las Vegas at any time, but Rory did request that you stay here until he returns. He wants to meet you. But first he needs to talk with Laurel and explain things. And as you know, she's going through a rough time. Although I might think Jack Aldrich is a bastard, Laurel thought she loved him."

Brooke backed down. "I'm sorry. You're right, I'm the one asking for a big favor." She was eager to meet her sister, but it was more than that. Thanks to her mother, she'd been alone all her life. She'd only been able to dream about having a family.

And if telling a white lie got her the opportunity, so be it. She wasn't leaving Colorado until she had a chance to make a connection, at least with her twin sister.

Chapter Four

An hour later, Brooke sat beside Trent in his truck, bumping along the winding dirt road that led to his ranch.

Grabbing hold of the safety handle to steady herself, she stole a glance across the bench seat to the man who suddenly had become her closest connection to her family. His clean-shaven jaw was set tight and his forehead furrowed in a deep frown, as if he were thinking about something serious. Was he her ally, or was he hoping she'd give up her quest and just leave Colorado?

She faced forward and concentrated on the incredible view. The lush green grass was waving in the warm autumn breeze while the cattle grazed in the pasture with the Rocky Mountains as a backdrop. It was like a different world here. A world she knew nothing about until two weeks ago, when she found the secrets hidden in Coralee's safety deposit box.

Suddenly she had a sister…and a father. And now she was on a ranch in Colorado waiting for her new family to come home.

Panic hit her. What if they wanted nothing to do with her? Didn't want her in their life? The familiar feeling of rejection caused an overwhelming ache in her chest.

Why should it matter whether Laurel or Rory Quinn accepted her? She'd been used to people turning their backs on her. Her mother was at the top of the list, unless she needed something. Even the men who'd walked in and out of Coralee's life over the years hated having a kid around.

When she was a child, her mom's career hadn't taken off yet, so Coralee had spent money on clothes to look nice for auditions. That meant they had to cut corners on other things like their apartment. So they ended up living in bad neighborhoods with slum apartments. A lot of them had been rent-by-the-week rooms with a kitchenette. Then there'd been the time when one of Coralee's boyfriends had stolen everything, including their money. She and her mother had had to go and live in shelters for a few weeks.

That had been the day Brooke decided she would never depend on anyone for anything, especially a man. She glanced at Trent. So what did she do? She was relying on a total stranger and letting him take her to his ranch.

She released a slow breath. What was going to happen when the whole truth about her came out?

"You're going to hurt yourself, thinking so hard."

Trent's voice pulled her back to the present.

"Sorry, I'm just worried about my mother," she lied. "She depends on me."

Trent glanced at her. "I thought she was in a care facility."

"She is, but I'm usually there nearly every day. I help her get bathed and dressed. She doesn't trust anyone else to do it."

His mesmerizing gaze locked on hers. "You must be pretty close."

"We've never had anyone else." She looked out the window. The beautiful scenery was distracting, but this man also had a strong pull.

"Your mother never married?"

She shook her head. "She was busy with her career. So it's always been just us," she said in a half truthful way. Men never stuck around for long. Had it been that way for Coralee with Rory Quinn? She'd asked her mother, but according to her, the man had been crazy about her.

God, was this a mistake to come here? Would Rory Quinn reject her when he learned that Coralee had lied to him about a second baby?

"Are you okay staying until Rory gets back here?"

She shrugged. "I'm sure there are other card dealers who are willing to take my shifts."

"And your mother?" he asked.

"I'll explain it to her. After all, it was Coralee who wanted me to come here."

"Good. Rory should be home in a couple of days."

"I probably should have called the Quinns before I drove all this way, but I thought—"

"You thought that Rory might tell you not to come," he finished for her.

She opened her mouth to deny it, but his words were true. "I'm still not sure what's going to happen."

"I've known Rory all my life. There isn't a mean bone in his body. He's a friend to everyone, and very generous. Besides, this only has to do with Laurel. She's an adult so it's her decision whether or not she wants a relationship with her sister."

Brooke wanted so badly to believe that. How about when they all learned the rest of the truth? Of course, she didn't expect Rory to immediately love her, but with her mother's debilitating illness it would be nice to have… someone. She felt the familiar tightness in her chest that reminded her of the years of loneliness.

She turned to Trent. "How well do you know Laurel?"

A smile appeared across his face. "Since they moved

here when Laurel was a baby. She was cute, and quite a little chatterbox. Then when I got older, she soon became a pain in the butt, following me around everywhere." His smiled faded as if he was thinking of something sad. "I moved away at fourteen and didn't see her much until I came back a few years ago."

Why did he move away so young? "So she's always lived here with her parents?"

He nodded. "Except for her years in college. She loves horses too much to leave the ranch permanently. And she's building a name for herself training quarter horses."

Trent glanced at Brooke's profile. He could see a strong resemblance between the two sisters. "That's the reason Rory wanted to build the cabins, the extra income would help Laurel get her dream of breeding and training her own horses."

He caught a trace of sadness in Brooke's green eyes. He doubted she'd lived an idyllic life back in Las Vegas. It couldn't have been easy for a single mother to raise a daughter alone. He hoped he'd find out more when Cody investigated Coralee. "Has your dream always been to work in the hotel business?" he asked, wanting to learn more.

She shrugged. "You can make a good living at it in Las Vegas, but I would prefer a smaller venue. That way you can give your guests a more personal touch."

He pulled up to the archway that read Lucky Bar L Ranch. "Be right back." He climbed out and swung open the metal gate, got back into the truck and drove through, then closed it again.

Further up the gravel road the two-story Landry house came into view. It had been freshly painted this past summer. Trent recalled the long hours he'd put in with a brush in his hand up high on a ladder. Come spring, the barn would be next to get a new coat.

He saw Brooke's interest as she looked around. "This is very nice."

"It's a work in progress. My dad was sick a long time and the place had gotten pretty run-down. I've been tackling as much as I can while keeping the ranch going."

She gave him a rare smile and suddenly his heart tripped.

"Your work has been worth it. The house looks lovely."

He pulled up in front of the barn. Going around the truck, he helped Brooke down from the high cab. His ranch hand, Rick Pierson, walked out to greet them.

"Hey, Trent," he called. "I didn't expect you back this morning." The twenty-two-year-old spoke to him, but his gaze was riveted on Brooke.

Why did that bother Trent? "I needed to check up on you to see if you're staying out of trouble."

"That's no fun." The part-time college student grinned, showing off those straight white teeth. He pushed his straw cowboy hat back and let his too-long blond hair fall across his forehead. Did the kid ever get a haircut?

"Don't worry, I've done all the chores, and Mike just rode out to check the herd."

"What about the downed fence by the creek?"

"When Mike gets back we'll head out to fix it. Unless we're needed for something else." He reached out a hand to Brooke. "Hi, I'm Rick Pierson."

She shook his hand. "Brooke Harper."

Rick didn't let go. "It's a pleasure to meet you. You're new in town."

Whoa, slow down, cowboy. "Brooke is here to see Laurel. And I'm capable of showing Miss Harper around wherever she needs to go."

The young boy faced off with him. "If you say so."

"I say so," Trent repeated. "Now, go load the truck up with the new fence posts I got in town the other day."

The kid's smile didn't waver as he tipped his hat. "It was nice to meet you, Brooke. Maybe I'll see you later."

She waved as he walked off. "Nice to meet you, too, Rick."

Trent sighed. "That boy flirts with every girl that gets within fifty feet of him. It surprises me he has time to work."

"He's just being friendly."

"I don't want Rick to make you feel uncomfortable."

She shook her head. "I work in a casino. I know when someone is flirting with me. Besides, I think he's charming."

Charming. He hadn't hired Rick to be charming. "You want to come up to the house, or would you like to look around?"

"Do you have horses?"

He nodded. "A few. Come on, I'll introduce you." He surprised himself when he grabbed her hand. Although he felt some resistance, she went with him into the barn.

Inside it was cooler, a little darker and smelled of hay and horse manure. Waiting for his eyes to adjust to the dim light, he looked around at the ten stalls. The new wood he'd used to rebuild most of them stood out, but as soon as he painted the rails no one could see the repairs.

He continued to hold her small hand and walked her over to the first stall and the seasoned mare, Cassie. He reached over the railing and the buckskin came to him immediately.

"Hey, girl." He rubbed her muzzle. "How you doing today?" She bobbed her head and blew out a warm breath. "I brought someone to meet you."

He glanced at Brooke to see her standing back, looking a little anxious. "Hey, this old girl is as gentle as they come. She would never hurt you. Castle Rock, better known as Cassie, this is Brooke." He reached for Brooke's hand and he had her stand on the bottom rung, then instructed her how to pet the horse.

"Oh, she's so soft," she said when her fingers came in contact with the horse's neck.

"She's just been bathed."

Cassie nuzzled her nose against Trent's arm as if to agree. He laughed. "She's pretty special to me."

Brooke's gaze met his. "Looks like she thinks you're pretty special, too."

He couldn't look away from the woman. "Yeah, we've been together a long time. My dad got her for me the first summer I came to visit him after my parents divorced. She was only a yearling then." Why was he telling her all this? He patted the horse's neck. "We're both getting up there."

"It's nice you still have her."

He nodded, unable to speak as good and bad memories flooded back. How he'd ride miles on Cassie, trying to outrun the memories of the brother he'd lost. He swallowed. "Yeah, she's been a good friend. Come on, I'll introduce you to the others."

They walked to the next stall and a large chestnut stallion came to the gate. "This is my mount, Red Baron." He took hold of the halter and held the horse's head steady. "He's a lot more spirited than Cassie."

"And you ride him?" she asked, keeping her distance.

Trying to avoid the horse's bobbing head, he admitted, "When he lets me. This guy keeps me on my toes." He rubbed the anxious stallion. "I need to take him out and give him a good run. Later I'll pasture him so he can run off some of his orneriness. I'd geld him, but first I want to get a few foals sired by him." He took her hand and walked down the aisle to the last stall and the small black mare with a white blaze on her face. "This is Raven. She's new to the Lucky Bar L. I've only had her a few months, and when she comes in season, I'll breed her with Red."

"So you're in the horse-breeding business."

"As a rancher, you need horses to run cattle. It's still the best way to round up the cows."

"This has to be a lot different than being in charge of soldiers."

He arched an eyebrow. "Actually sometimes the steers take commands better."

He saw her smile and his gut tightened. Whoa. This was not the time for him to take notice of a woman. Not this woman, anyway.

TWENTY MINUTES LATER, in the nineteen-fifties-style kitchen, Brooke sat across the table from Trent eating a ham sandwich and drinking iced tea. She couldn't stop looking around in amazement.

Although the cabinets where old, they were painted a high glossy white and the tiled counters were a tan with a burgundy trim. A soft yellow covered the walls. The appliances were original, too, but fit in with the decor. This was how she always thought a family kitchen should look.

"I know this room needs to be redone, but right now, it's on the bottom of my list."

"Oh, no. This kitchen is amazing as it is. I was just admiring the great condition of everything."

"You can thank my dad. He was the original recycler, and believed in taking care of things he had. He worked hard at ranching and hated to waste anything." Trent took a bite of his sandwich. "Since there were so many other repairs on my list, I could only paint the walls and cabinets for now."

"And you did an excellent job." She smiled. "With running a ranch and now, the cabins to build, you must be pretty busy."

"Well, since Aldrich took off with the money, it seems the cabins are on hold until we decide what to do."

And here she was adding to Rory and Trent's problems. "Then I show up."

He paused, his gaze locked on hers. "You have nothing to do with our troubles."

"No, but I'm adding more, especially for Laurel. Probably the last thing she needs right now is to learn about her…mother."

Trent took a drink of tea. "Honestly, I don't know how she'll react to the news. But you drove all this way to meet Laurel, so sticking around a few days is better than going home without trying to connect, isn't it?"

She wasn't sure about that. "Yeah, but look at all the time I'm taking from you. You're stuck babysitting me until the Quinns get home."

He leaned back in the chair, and she couldn't help noticing his muscular chest and those massive shoulders. Did the military do that for him, or the ranch work?

He caught her stare and she quickly glanced away.

"Hey, I'll take your kind of trouble any day. You rescued me yesterday by helping me pack up all that wedding stuff. You took charge yesterday like a drill sergeant."

She felt a blush cover her cheeks. "What can I say? I have a knack for getting things done."

Those dark eyes captured her attention for far too long. She couldn't let this man get to her. Once he learned the truth about her, he might not like that she'd kept it from him.

He rested his elbows on the table. "Have you ever ridden?"

She swallowed hard. "You mean on a horse?"

He gave her an odd look, but she could tell he was trying not to laugh. "Yes, as far as I'm concerned, it's the best way to see the countryside."

"You want to take me riding?"

"You seem surprised. I'm sure your sister will want to show you around, too."

"To be honest, I've never been on or around a horse until today."

Brooke's first instinct was to say no, but then she realized she'd never taken time just for herself. And why wouldn't she want to go riding with this rugged cowboy? "I'll go, but only if you put me on a gentle horse. You've got one named Poky or Snail?"

"Don't worry, I'll make sure you're safe."

She wanted to believe him, but something deep told her if she wasn't careful she could get hurt, and in more ways than one.

Chapter Five

Thirty minutes later in the corral, with a borrowed cowboy hat on her head, Brooke sat atop Cassie as Trent adjusted her stirrups. She released a shallow breath to keep calm, but this horse was really big. Looking down, she discovered she was also far from the ground. Maybe this wasn't a good idea.

Trent glanced up at her from under the brim of his cowboy hat. "How does that feel?"

"Okay, I guess."

"Stand up," he instructed, then did another adjustment before he handed her the reins. When she held the leather straps in a death grip, his gloved hand covered hers. "Relax. I won't let anything happen to you."

Oddly, his calming voice made her want to believe him. "Easy for you to say," she tried to tease and the animal under her shifted. She gasped.

"Whoa there, darlin'," he crooned to the horse.

"I thought you said she was gentle."

"Cassie's just happy she's getting out of the barn. I've been spending a lot of time at the Bucking Q with the cabin construction."

After a quick pat on the mare's neck, he walked to a rust-colored gelding named Rango. Taking the reins, he grabbed the horn, jammed his boot into the stirrup, then swung his leg over the horse and sat down in the saddle. He wheeled the horse around and rode him around the pen, and began showing her different commands.

She wasn't sure she could remember any of them because she was too distracted by the man on the horse. Trent Landry was impressive.

"Just stay close to me," he said as he rode up to her. "Cassie won't run off."

Run off? Brooke swallowed hard and felt the horse shift under her again. She tensed.

"Relax, Brooke. This is supposed to be fun."

Fun? She couldn't remember the last time she'd just had fun. She nodded. "If you say so."

He grinned. "You're going to do fine." He covered her hands with his. "Remember, relax your hold."

She did as he asked.

"That's better. Come on, let's go and see some of Colorado up close." He walked his horse toward the gate.

"Okay, girl," Brooke began, "It's time to go." Cassie didn't move right away. Instead, the seasoned mare swung her large head around, then finally gave a nod. Brooke couldn't help smiling as Cassie started off.

After a while Brooke began relax into the rhythm of the animal as the trail wandered through a grove of white birch trees. The sun streamed through the foliage, dotting the landscape with light as they made their way toward the foothills.

Drawing in a breath of the mountain air, she let the scent of pine and damp earth fill her nostrils. She looked toward the pasture to see cattle grazing. Some of the bovines raised their heads as if to say hi, then went back to feeding. There was a cute white-faced calf running around the herd as if trying to get someone to play.

Brooke couldn't stop looking at the striking scenery, or

comparing it to the desert where she'd grown up. Such a contrast. Suddenly she realized she was enjoying herself and got a silly grin on her face. She barely refrained from shouting, "Hey, look at me, I'm riding a horse."

When the trail widened, Trent dropped back and rode beside her. He smiled. "Like some company?"

She tried not to tense up, but this man looked good on a horse, decked out in his Stetson hat and boots. Who was she kidding? Trent Landry would look good even without the cowboy props.

"Sure," she managed.

They rode along in silence, then he began pointing out some landmarks. What she really wanted was to ask questions about Laurel, also Rory. Yet she didn't want to give herself away. If Trent discovered her secret, he might not be so willing to let her stay and meet the man she'd never gotten a chance to call father.

Laurel's childhood had been so different from hers. Brooke couldn't help wondering if they could ever find common ground, maybe become friends...even sisters. She felt a rush of emotion, thinking about her lonely years growing up.

"You're looking pretty serious again," Trent said.

She blinked, feeling the blush rise to her cheeks. "Sorry, I guess I get a little intense sometimes. It's hard to turn it off. My job is pretty stressful."

Trent held the reins loosely in his hand and the horses walked slowly along the grassy trail. The easy rocking in the saddle was soothing. She could get used to this.

"And taking care of your mother can't be easy, either."

Brooke quickly came back to reality. "She has her good days."

"She's probably happy to have you there with her."

Was she? Brooke had never been sure how Coralee felt.

They'd never had the typical mother-daughter relationship. And now with the disease destroying her mother's mind, she would never know. "I think she's worried about seeing Laurel."

He nodded. "Well, it can't be easy to give up a child."

And not tell the father that there were two babies. "No, it probably wasn't, but I guess Coralee had her reasons. I just didn't know them."

Trent gave a sideways glance toward Brooke. He was still trying to figure her out. Why did she call her mother Coralee sometimes? His instincts told him there was something she wasn't telling him. As much as Rory seemed to distrust Coralee, Trent couldn't help thinking there might be something else going on.

He stole another glance at the pretty blonde's profile, seeing more and more of a resemblance to Laurel. Although unlike Laurel, he didn't feel toward Brooke.

About fifteen minutes later, they came up on a creek, and Cassie quickly veered off the trail, heading in the direction of the water.

"Hey, whoa." Brooke tugged on the reins and looked back at Trent. "Why isn't she stopping?"

He followed after them. "It's okay. Just let her go, she's thirsty. I think we all could use something to drink."

Trent could see Brooke put slack in the reins and let the horse take her through the trees to the rocky edge. He was impressed with the way she sat in the saddle. It had taken a little while, but she'd finally let the tension ease and sat back to enjoy the ride. He wished he could say the same of himself. He felt the awareness in full alert whenever he got close to her.

Once beside the creek under a large shade tree, the horses began to drink at the rocky edge. Trent went to Brooke, instructing her how to dismount. She managed to swing her leg over the saddle, but he didn't think she realized the long distance to the ground, or that her legs wouldn't hold her up. With her sudden cry, Trent gripped her by the waist.

"I got you," he told her as he steadied her. "It's not unusual to feel a little shaky."

"I didn't realize my leg muscles would turn to mush. We haven't been riding that long."

Trent inhaled her soft scent and his body reacted quickly. "Riding isn't as easy as it looks, and this is your first time on a horse."

"So the next time will be easier?" she asked as she looked at him from under her cowboy hat. Her big green eyes looked both leery and hopeful at the same time.

"Maybe after a good long soak in a tub."

Aw, hell, why did he go and say that? Suddenly he conjured up a picture of her naked, covered in bubbles... He glanced away and helped her to the water's edge. Once Brooke was seated, he went and checked the horses, then pulled a retractable tin cup from his saddlebag.

"Here, use this."

She took the small cup. "Thank you." She dipped it into the cool stream to fill it, then took a drink. "Oh, this is so good."

Her deep moan caused another reaction he didn't expect. He pushed his hat back. "No need for bottled water around here."

She scooped up another cupful and his gaze was riveted on watching her long, slender neck as she swallowed thirstily. He fought to keep from reaching out and wiping the water that trickled down her flushed cheek. Once finished, she quickly ran her hand across her mouth and collected any traces of leftover liquid.

"Guess I was thirstier than I thought," Brooke said as

she removed her hat and brushed her hair away from her face, exposing the dusting of freckles across her nose. She turned toward him and looked serious. "Something wrong? Is there dirt on my face?"

"No." Quickly he crouched down at the creek's edge, cupped his hands, and concentrated on drinking the cool water. After his fill, he sat down next to her. Maybe not a good idea. He eyed her long legs encased in those slim-fitting jeans. He was far too aware of this woman, and that wasn't good for either of them. Maybe he shouldn't work all the time, just find himself a woman to go out with.

Brooke interrupted his thoughts. "You have a pretty impressive backyard, Mr. Landry. Thank you for sharing it with me today."

"You're welcome." Trent readjusted his hat and stared out at the mountain range as a breeze rustled through the trees. He noticed the leaves were beginning to turn autumn colors, his favorite time of year. "I've probably explored about every cave and mesa around this property. My dad wanted to make sure his boys knew how to handle themselves."

"Boys? You have a brother?"

He cursed under his breath for the slip. "Yeah. My younger brother...Chris." Even though it had been nearly twenty years, a sharp pain sliced through his chest as if the accident had happened yesterday.

"Does he live around here?"

More pain, he swallowed hard. "No, he died a long time ago."

He couldn't look at her, but heard her gasp. "Oh, Trent, I'm so sorry."

He could only nod as the details of that day flooded back. He shook them away and stood. "We should head back." He went to retrieve their mounts.

Brooke followed him and placed her hand on his arm. "I'm sorry if I brought up some bad memories."

He saw the sadness on her face. Although he didn't deserve it, he wanted to take the comfort she offered. "There are no good memories when a young boy dies."

Not when his older brother didn't have the time to watch out for him.

AFTER RETURNING FROM their ride, Trent took care of the horses, then he spoke with Ricky about the chores for the next day before he drove Brooke back to the Bucking Q. After dropping her off at the cabin, he drove next door, relieved that she hadn't asked him any more questions about Chris.

Still angry, he climbed out and slammed the truck door. Damn. He hadn't talked about what happened to his brother in years. Why now? And with a virtual stranger? Not that the incident had been a secret. Anyone in town who knew them could probably tell her about Chris's tragic accident. But he didn't want to dredge up memories of the awful day that still ate away at his gut.

Once inside, Trent closed the door and ran a hand over his face. He'd spent years trying to rid himself of the demons that followed him even after he moved away to Denver with his mother. Then there was guilt over his parents' divorce because Wade and Leslie Landry couldn't get over their young son's death.

He could still remember the endless silence in the house that had once been so full of laughter with two rambunctious boys. His chest tightened as the raw emotions nearly strangled him.

For years, the pain of coming back to the Lucky Bar L had been agonizing. He'd only returned when he was younger because the court ordered it, but he had trouble facing his father. He hated seeing the sadness in Wade's eyes. He hated that he'd let his father down by not watching out for his brother.

After graduating high school, Trent had gone straight into the army. He'd wanted to do something worthwhile. Maybe he could help save lives to pay for the brother he couldn't save.

A sob formed in his throat, nearly choking him. "Dammit. I'm not doing this now."

He needed a distraction. He walked across the room, pulled out his phone and punched in Cody Marsh's number. Surely the PI had some news for him.

Maybe it was his years of military training but he couldn't help feeling there was something Brooke wasn't telling. Okay, he was suspicious by nature. And he wanted to know more about Brooke Harper. Of course she looked too much like Laurel not to be her half sister, but... There were too many buts.

"Hey, Rocky, how it's going on the ranch?"

Trent smiled at the familiar nickname that had been with him since boot camp. Since he lived in the Rocky Mountains, the men had deemed it just right for him.

"You tell me, Swamp Man." With Cody's last name being Marsh, and him coming from Florida, this had seemed the perfect moniker for him. "You got any news for me?"

"Some. Concerning Aldrich, there's no police record, but he'd been married and was divorced about three years ago. Financially, he's in debt up to his eyebrows. Some of his credit card charges show that he frequents the casinos around Denver. My guess is he took off with your money since he was being chased by the not-so-nice guys. Word is he owes money to the wrong people."

Trent cursed. He hated to think that Laurel could have been mixed up in that mess.

"Now, for Coralee Harper. She's been a resident of Las Vegas for thirty-two years. Over the years, she's had numerous addresses and jobs, but hasn't been employed since 2014. She now resides at the Carlton Caring House as an Alzheimer's patient."

"Did you find anything about her having daughters?" Trent asked.

"If she did, they weren't born in Las Vegas. Coralee does have a daughter listed as a contact, Brooke Marie Harper. But I haven't had a chance to check into Brooke's history yet." There was a tired sigh. "Sorry, Rocky, I've been working nonstop another case, and I'll be off grid doing surveillance for the next forty-eight hours. I can hook you up with another PI, but that's the soonest I can get back to you."

Trent didn't like the delay, but he doubted Rory would be back in town before then, anyway.

"No, I can wait. I'll talk to you then. Thanks, man." Trent disconnected the call and slipped his phone in his pocket.

He walked into the cabin's kitchenette. It was identical to the one Brooke was staying in, and there wasn't much. He opened the refrigerator and saw beer, milk and a carton of eggs. There wasn't much more in the cupboards. His appetite suddenly disappeared.

He checked his phone for any messages from Rory, but he knew he wouldn't hear from him until at least tomorrow. Hopefully by then, he'd say they were on their way home. Then he could return to the Lucky Bar L and get on with business and forget about Brooke Harper.

He walked to the window and glanced out at the unfinished cabins off in the distance. He needed to come up with a way to complete the construction. The longer they sat like this, the more money they were losing.

He checked his watch. There was about thirty minutes before the bank closed. Taking out his phone, he got the number from information and was connected to the loan department. When he ended the call, he had a three o'clock appointment with a Mr. Jason Parks to discuss another loan. A loan that might not pan out. His original investment in the hunting and fishing cabins had come from his savings. Years in the army allowed him to be able to build up quite a savings. That and the fact he'd invested in the stock market.

He shook his head. Although he'd known the time was right to retire from the military, he still wasn't sure the ranch was home for him. But he hadn't been looking for a home in a very long time. Could Hidden Springs be that place? Again?

BROOKE SAT ON the leather sofa in the cabin, her phone to her ear, listening as the care facility director and owner, Erin Carlton, went over her mother's bad day.

Not good.

Then her mother came on the line. "Brooke, tell me all about Laurel," Coralee crooned into the phone, her voice raspy from years of drinking and smoking. "Is she beautiful? I know she's pretty because even as a baby she looked like me."

Coralee never told Brooke she was pretty. She should be used to her mother's indifference, but the words still stung. "I haven't had a chance to meet her yet, Mother."

"Is Rory keeping her from you?" Her anger was evident. "I bet he's saying bad things about me. Don't let him, Brooke. I had to give Laurel away. She was too sick for me to handle."

"I know, Mother. And you had your career."

"It was my chance to audition for the Golden Palace show with Jessica Bright. I know I was only one of the backup singers, but I could have got discovered." Her voice was teary. "Now, I need to see Laurel. I have to tell her why I gave her away. Please help me, Brooke. If you love me you'll find her."

A knife pierced Brooke's heart. She should be used to her mother's selfishness, but it never ceased to hurt.

"I'm doing the best I can."

Coralee began to cry. "Please, I need to see her."

Brooke closed her eyes and heard a soothing voice talking with her mother, then Erin came back on the line. "Sorry about that, Brooke. Carol is putting Coralee to bed."

"Erin, should I drive back?"

"No, your mother is doing fine, and although she's been restless most of the day, she's been lucid ." There was a pause, then Erin went on to remind her, "We've discussed this, Brooke. Coralee's confusion and her frustration and anger are all part of the disease. And add in the possibility of seeing the daughter she gave away… It's a lot to handle."

Even before the Alzheimer's took over, her mother could be difficult. "I wish I had some news for her, but Rory and Laurel are out of town. They won't be back until tomorrow, or maybe the day after that."

"Then Coralee will have to deal with that," Erin told her.

Erin was only a few years older than Brooke, and they had quickly become friends over the past six months. Erin was a nurse working in a hospital until her military husband, Jarred, returned from deployment permanently disabled. Unable to leave him, she'd turned their home into a care facility. At the house Erin had also cared for her wheelchair-bound husband until his death a few months ago. Brooke felt blessed that she'd found a place for Coralee there.

"Do you have a place to stay?"

"Yes, I'm actually staying at the ranch in one of the fishing cabins, so I'm saving some money."

"But you haven't talked with Rory?"

"No, their neighbor Trent Landry is Rory's partner." She went on to tell her about the hunting and fishing business and a little bit about Laurel's quarter-horse training.

"Sounds like a nice guy."

And good-looking. Brooke thought about the man who'd taken her horseback riding today. She also couldn't forget the sadness in his voice when he'd talked about his brother. "He's retired army, Special Forces master sergeant."

Erin chuckled. "So a real hard-ass, huh."

"I wouldn't call him that. He's been nice to let me stay here."

"Oh, sounds like you've taken notice of the man. I bet he's good-looking, in a military and cowboy sort of way. Lucky you."

Before Brooke could deny anything to her friend, a knock sounded. "I've got to go, Erin, there's someone at the door."

"Hey, make sure you ask who it is."

"Yes, ma'am, I will. Tell Coralee I'll talk to her soon. Good night."

Brooke walked to the door and pulled it partway open to find Trent standing on her porch. He was dressed in a black collared shirt and fresh jeans stacked on shiny black boots, and the familiar cowboy hat on his head. Her heart raced, but knew this was the last man she needed to be attracted to. "Trent. Is something wrong?"

"Yeah, I'm hungry and was wondering if you'd like to go into town with me to get something to eat."

Okay, that was the last thing she expected to come out of his mouth. She started to deny she was hungry when her stomach chose that moment to give a very unlady-like growl.

He cocked an eyebrow at her, and her heart did another happy dance. "I take it that's a yes."

Chapter Six

Brooke felt the heat rise to her cheeks. So embarrassing. "Sorry. I guess I forgot all about the time. I was planning on fixing a sandwich and going to bed early."

Trent gave cocked an eyebrow at her. "Are you sore from the ride?"

"Not too bad. I took aspirin earlier and I'm feeling a lot better now."

She stepped back and allowed him inside. It was the polite thing to do. She couldn't help noticing him, especially since he smelled so good. Not with a heavy cologne, but with the clean fragrance of soap and what was becoming familiar to her as Trent's scent. He had on a clean pair of jeans and a Western shirt tucked into that narrow waist.

He was what women called the total package, but cowboy-style. She noticed his wide belt with a buckle that showed off some kind of lettering. She looked up to see him watching her.

"It's the Lucky Bar L brand." He pointed to his buckle. "See the horseshoe, with the bar and the L? It was my dad's favorite."

He smiled at her and her heart tripped. She hated that she kept reacting to this man. "Impressive."

"So was my dad." He glanced away, then changed the subject. "So how about some supper?"

She released a breath. "I can't keep taking up your time, Trent. Surely you have better things to do than baby-sit me, especially when I don't need it. Really, I'm fine here by myself."

"If you're worried about me having other things to do, I can tell you right now, I don't. I mean, there's roundup next week, but that's not tonight. I was going into town anyway to eat at this barbecue place that has the best ribs anywhere. I just thought you might like to go. If not, I guess I can go alone."

When he started for the door, Brooke stopped him. "You're really going into town?"

He turned and nodded. "You bet. Their secret family sauce is definitely worth the fifteen-mile trip. I've been around the world, and Joe's barbecue sauce is the best I've tasted. Mouthwatering with beef or pork."

She started laughing and held up her hands. "Okay, okay. You've sold me. I'll go."

"You sure? I don't want to pressure you." She could see he was fighting a grin.

"No pressure at all." She went to get her purse off the coffee table. "But I'm paying my way."

"We'll see about that."

She stopped suddenly, turned around to agree and ran into the solid wall of Trent's chest. She gasped as he gripped her by the arms to steady her, just as her palms pressed against his muscular body. She raised her head and caught a gleam in his chocolate eyes.

She quickly removed her hands. "Sorry, I didn't mean to run you down."

He didn't let go of her right way. "Darlin', you'd have to pack on another hundred pounds to do any damage."

He was the type of man who could easily distract her from the reason she was here. She never had time to flirt with men, or much desire, after seeing her mother in action. "I'll remember that."

He winked. "Just letting you know that you didn't hurt me."

She quickly stepped back and headed toward the door. "Come, let's get some of that barbecue you've been boasting about." She grabbed her jacket, and Trent opened the door and they went out to the porch.

"Joe's lives up to the hype. As soon as we get there, I can prove my point."

Once at his truck, he opened the door, then proceeded to lift her into the high seat. "I didn't ask, because you'd probably argue about my helping you." He grumbled something about independent women before he closed the door.

Brooke smiled to herself. It was nice to have a man take charge for a change and do something for her. Yet, she'd learned the hard way that she was better off being independent and self-sufficient.

The handsome cowboy opened the driver's-side door and climbed in. No matter how handsome, she had to stop reacting to him. She had no idea how things here would turn out when the Quinns came home. She could get thrown off the property, or would they open their arms to her?

She looked across the cab to Trent. He didn't know the entire truth about her, and right now, she didn't know him well enough to reveal the complicated story. She wasn't even sure if she could tell Rory. Right now her concern was to bring Laurel back to Las Vegas to see Coralee.

Twenty minutes later, Trent arrived with Brooke at Joe's Barbecue Smoke House. The spicy aroma greeted him first, then the noise as they stepped through the double doors. The large restaurant was always packed on a Sunday. A lot of families filled the large picnic-style tables and high-back booths. In a separate room, there was a long wooden bar lined with patrons, watching the several televisions playing the football game. You could also hear in the background the familiar voice of George Strait singing "Ace in the Hole."

Then another group of people came in the door, pushing Trent forward into Brooke. His body brushed against hers, immediately making him aware of her nice curves.

He leaned down toward her ear and whispered, "Sorry. I forgot how crowded this place gets on the weekend."

She shivered and he stood close enough to see the goose bumps rise along her slender neck. How would she taste if he pressed his lips there? He blinked and pulled back. Damn. This was only dinner, and she wasn't on the menu.

She turned to him. "It's okay. I have a feeling, with the wonderful aroma, the food is worth it."

Right, think about the barbecue ribs.

Suddenly Trent heard his name. He glanced up to see Joe McClain rushing through the crowded room. The tall man dressed in a chef's apron had a big grin on his face. "Hey, long time no see, buddy."

They hugged. "Sorry, I've been busy."

"So, how are the cabins coming?" Joe asked.

Trent shook his head. "Pretty slow right now." He didn't want to get into the details. He put his hand against Brooke's back. "Joe, this is Brooke Harper. She's visiting for a few days. I thought I'd bring her into town for some good food."

Joe smiled as he looked at Brooke. "Nice to meet you, Brooke."

She nodded. "Nice to meet you, too, Joe."

Joe studied her. "You must be related to the Quinns, because you sure look like Laurel. And you're just as pretty."

"Stop the flirting," Trent said, hating that his friend was showing interest. He tried to lighten the mood. "At least until you find us a table."

Joe laughed. "Let me see what I can do." He called the hostess over and instructed her to find a couple of seats. He turned back to Brooke. "Sorry about the wedding fiasco, but I can't say I'm sad that Laurel didn't marry that jerk. She deserves better."

Brooke nodded since it was nearly impossible to speak over all the noise. A hostess escorted them into the bar area, toward the back wall next to the fireplace. Outside of a few cheers and groans from the bar over the football game, it was quieter then the dinning room.

Once seated across from Brooke, Trent placed his arms on the table and leaned forward. "At least now I can hear what you have to say. Remind me to thank Joe."

"Yes, we should definitely thank him," she repeated and opened the menu.

Trent stopped her, putting his hand over hers. "No need to even look at that. Just get the sampler rib platter and you can have a little bit of everything."

"But what if there are some things I don't like?"

He shrugged. "I'll eat what you don't like."

Brooke was working hard to keep her breathing slow… relaxed, but with Trent's hand covering hers, it was difficult. She finally slipped her hand away. "That's so much food."

"That's the best part, they have a small and a large size platter."

A young waitress about twenty-five walked over to the table. "Hi, Trent. It's been a long time."

"Hi, Jenna. How's school going?"

The pretty brunette sighed. "Hard, but I'm getting through."

"It's worth it, so stay in college."

"Yeah, I don't want to work here all my life, especially with my brother as my boss. He lets me work around my classes, so I guess he's not so bad."

"Well, congratulations," Trent said, then made the introductions. "Jenna, this is Brooke Harper. Brooke, this is Joe's sister, Jenna McClain. She goes to nursing school up the road."

"Hi, Brooke." The girl looked at her curiously, making Brooke a little nervous. "You sure look like Laurel. Are you a cousin or something?"

Brooke had no idea what to say. "Or something."

Trent saved her. "Hey, Jenna, do you think you can rustle us up some food?

She pulled out her order pad. "Sure, what would you like?"

"Two sampler platters, one large and the other small. And two draft beers." He arched an eyebrow at Brooke and she nodded at his choices.

Jenna picked up the menus. "Beers will be over as soon as Harry can pour them."

"Not a problem," he said.

After the waitress walked away, Trent looked at her. "You sure you're okay with the beer?"

The truth was she wasn't much of a drinker, but she could handle one beer. "Sounds good with all those ribs I'm going to be eating."

He leaned back in his chair, crossed his arms over his massive chest and studied her with a piercing gaze. She worked to keep her breathing calm, but this man could intimidate anyone.

"It doesn't hurt to indulge every once in a while," he told her. "As I used to tell my recruits, just don't overdo it."

"If I'm going to indulge on anything, I would rather it be on chocolate."

A wide grin transformed his face, causing warmth to spread through her, and settling deep in her stomach.

"What is it with women and chocolate?"

She could play this game, for a while, anyway. She leaned forward, and looked him in the eye. "If you have to ask, then my telling you isn't going to help."

When he frowned, she couldn't help laughing.

The bartender brought over two beers. Trent thanked him, then lifted his glass toward Brooke. "To a night hearing more of your sweet laughter."

Brooke swallowed. She couldn't let Trent's words turn her head. "Oh, my, you're full of blarney, Mr. Landry." She took a long drink of her beer to cool off. "And you aren't even Irish."

He tipped his head back and laughed. "What about you, Miss Harper? Do you have any Irish in you?"

Brooke gripped her glass, playing with the condensation. "Don't we all claim to be part Irish?"

Before he could answer her, two platters arrived at the table. All she could do was groan on seeing the stacks of ribs on her plate. "Looks like I'm going to have enough leftovers for several days."

"Not me." Trent rubbed his hands together, then tore off the first rib and took a big bite. Then he released a deep groan and something stirred in Brooke's stomach. Need. Want. Desire.

She quickly looked down at her plate, picked up her own rib and took a bite. Her taste buds went nuts. "Oh, my Lord, this is so good. Sweet and tangy at the same time."

"Told you," Trent said.

She couldn't help thinking back to the years when things had been really tight for her and her mother. There'd been times when they hadn't had enough to eat. And never could her mother afford a meal like this.

Over the next twenty minutes, they both were more interested in the food rather than conversation. But eating ribs was messy. Brooke kept trying to clean her hands off with her napkin. Hard to do when she couldn't resist gnawing the tender meat all the way to the bone.

Trent couldn't help watching Brooke as she enjoyed her meal. Although she had no problem digging into the ribs, she did it in a way that intrigued him. She had quite an appetite. He couldn't help wondering what other things she enjoyed.

Yesterday, she'd taken charge of dismantling a wedding reception like a pro. Then today, on horseback, even though she was afraid, she wouldn't let that keep her from learning to ride. But now…one on one, she seemed almost shy with him, especially when he tried to give her compliments. Maybe she had spent all her time with her career and her mother, and hadn't had much time for socializing. She hadn't mentioned a boyfriend.

He studied her pretty face. Her complexion was creamy smooth, and those incredible green eyes… His libido kicked into overdrive. All right, he was attracted to her, but he couldn't let that distract him from finding out more about her and her mother.

She looked at him as her tongue snaked out and licked sauce from her full lips. "Is something wrong?" she asked innocently.

He managed to hold back his groan as he leaned forward, reached out and wiped barbecue sauce off her cheek. "Just a little something the napkin missed." When his fingers made contact with her skin, he had trouble concentrating. She was as soft as he imagined.

She didn't pull back but her face turned rosy red. "As my mother used to say, you can't take me anywhere." She forced a laugh to hide her embarrassment. ·

Why would she say that? "I like to watch a woman enjoy her food."

"Maybe because I enjoy eating so much. I had to grab food when I had the chance." She rushed on to say, "Between school and working."

He bet there was a lot more to that story. "I've never been known to miss a meal, not growing up, anyway. And there's something about home cooking that is hard to resist."

She sat back and wiped off her hands with her napkin. "I wouldn't know since cooking wasn't Coralee's strong suit."

"What was your mother good at?"

"Singing. At one time she had a beautiful voice. And a lot of promise to make it big time." She sighed. "So many things robbed her of her chance for the spotlight."

"Surely you don't blame yourself for your mother's failures."

She shook her head. "At first I used to, but no, Coralee made her own bad choices. And those years took a toll."

He found he wanted to hear more. "What about your father? Was he in your life?"

Her eyes widened at his question, and she quickly shook her head.

"That's rough. It's not easy being a single mother. I know after my parents divorced, my mother had to go to work. Everything changed."

"That had to be an adjustment for you."

"Not as bad as when she remarried." He thought back

to the day his mother had brought a man named Neal Brannigan to their apartment.

"You have a stepfather?"

He nodded. "We all lived together, along with my twin stepbrothers. One big happy family."

Her eyes widened. "Twins?"

He nodded. "Believe me, Austin and Cullen were double trouble, and didn't want much to do with me, either."

Her soft voice drew him back to the present. "I take it you didn't get along."

He shrugged and took a drink of his beer, realizing it was warm. "At first, no. But by the time I left for the army, we developed a healthy respect for each other."

"At least you have a family."

His gaze locked on hers, and he couldn't miss the sadness in her eyes. There was a nagging feeling that his life with the Brannigan brothers was a cakewalk compared to hers. *What are your secrets, Brooke Harper?* One thing for sure, he needed to remember why she came to Hidden Springs. She might be here to meet her sister, but at what cost to the Quinn family?

THE DRIVE HOME was quiet, causing Brooke to feel a little nervous. Had she said too much? Should she have just told Trent the truth about Rory being her father? Would he even believe her now?

She thought about the birth certificate tucked in the pocket of her suitcase. Coralee had named Rory Quinn as father to both her and Laurel. Sharing the same birthday with Laurel proved they were twins.

"Have I bored you to death and you've fallen asleep?" Trent asked.

She looked at him. "Just so full from the meal, it's hard to breathe, let alone talk. And I'm enjoying the quiet."

Trent turned off the highway and through the gate. Without the truck's headlights, the road would be pitch-black.

"I'm sure this is quite a change from the bright lights you're used to."

"It is. I mostly worked nights and went to school during the day, so this solid darkness is a little overwhelming to me. I'm glad you know where you're going."

"I guess being raised out here I'm used to the darkness, but yeah, I like it better with moonlight."

There was something in his voice that made her ask, "I bet coming home is nice after being deployed overseas."

The road was bumpy, and Trent slowed the truck. "Yeah, it's nice being back. I wished I'd come home more. I hadn't seen my dad in a lot of years, and for that I'm ashamed. That's something I'll always regret. Wade Landry was a good man, and he deserved a better son."

She heard the emotion in his voice. "Oh, Trent, how can you say that? You were a young boy who had to leave here… Your parents' divorce was hard on you, too."

"My dad used to write me letters when I was deployed, but he never said anything about being sick. I don't think he even told Rory." He stole a glance at her. "They were best friends."

"Your father probably didn't want you to worry about him. You had a job to do, and being distracted by his illness might have put you in jeopardy."

Trent pulled up in front of the cabins and shut off the engine, but he didn't get out. He turned to her, and with the aid of the porch light, she could see the intensity in his eyes.

"That's what Rory told me when I came home for Dad's funeral."

"Then believe him, Trent. I also think your father would be happy to know you came home to stay."

With a nod, Trent climbed out of the truck then came around and helped her down. He took her hand and walked her to the porch. "Thanks for tonight, Brooke. You saved a lonely old soldier from a solitary meal."

"Oh, yeah, you're really old. What, thirty?"

"Thirty-three," he corrected.

"Well, get out the cane then."

He smiled at her and her heart began to race once again, then he grew serious as he leaned closer toward her. "I guess I should let you get some sleep. I need some shut-eye, too. I have to ride out to check the herd early in the morning."

"Are you going far?"

"A few miles to the north pasture. We need to bring them closer to the pens so we can do the branding."

Why did she want to go? She could barely sit on a horse. "Sounds like fun."

He cocked an eyebrow. "You didn't get enough today?"

"I really enjoy the ride."

"Well then, if you can be up and ready by five, you're welcome to go along."

She blinked at the invitation. "You're kidding, right? You're inviting me along?"

He grinned. "Who am I to cheat you out of all that fun?"

Chapter Seven

At 5:00 a.m. the next morning, the sun wasn't even up. Good thing Brooke had always been an early riser. At twelve, she'd had a paper route, using the extra money from her payments to make sure that there was food.

Even if Coralee had made good tips at whatever bar she'd worked, she didn't always come home with the money. Sometimes she went out and partied, or met some guy and spent it on alcohol or drugs.

Brooke shook away the bad memories and pulled a long-sleeved shirt over her head. Aware of the low temperature, she slipped on her hooded sweatshirt for another layer when she heard a soft knock on the door. Her heart suddenly skipped a beat knowing Trent was on the other side, and she would be spending the day with him.

"Stop fantasizing about a man you can't have. Besides, you wouldn't know what to do with him if you had the chance," she murmured, then opened the door and felt the cool air hit her. She needed it seeing the handsome man taking up space in the doorway.

"Mornin'," he said, then smiled at her and stole her breath.

"Good morning," she managed as she stepped aside and allowed him inside.

"I wasn't sure if you were serious about going today."

"I'm used to getting up early." She noticed his hands were full. "With going to school and my job, I had to be."

He nodded and held out a pair of boots. "Here, I scrounged up a pair of Laurel's. They aren't the cleanest, but at least your feet will have some protection."

She eyed the worn brown leather, but the tooling on the sides made them look expensive. "I don't want to wear them without her permission."

"Laurel isn't going to care. They're just an old pair of barn boots. Do you know what that means?" He grinned. "She mucks out stalls and bathes horses in them. And today, they're going to protect your feet around the cattle and horses."

Brooke finally took the prize he offered. "Thank you." She went to the sofa, removed her sneakers then slipped on the first boot over her sock, then its mate. She stood and walked around.

"It'll take a little while to get used to walking in them," Trent said. "Do they rub anywhere?"

She shook her head. "My socks are pretty thick."

She looked at him. He was wearing a camel-colored jacket with sheepskin lining that made him seem even larger than he was. He had on his black Stetson and she noticed the dark shadow of his beard along his jaw.

His gaze caught hers. "I also found you a coat. It's cold out, so don't think about arguing over this, because I don't want to hear it."

"I won't." Grateful, she took the jacket and slipped it on. It was a little big, but fit her well enough. "It feels…warm."

He nodded and placed a hat on her head. "Now let's go. I've trailered the horses to take up to the pasture."

Brooke put a few things in her pockets—cell phone, a granola bar and tissue—then hurried to catch up with him as he was already off the porch and headed toward the truck and trailer.

"Will I be riding Cassie again?"

He helped her into the raised truck. "No, it's a harder ride than I'd like for her, and I want you on a sturdier mount."

Once inside the cab, he handed her a foil-wrapped package. "Here, eat this."

"I already had some fruit and toast."

"You need the calories today." He drove through the gate, but instead of heading to the highway, he took a narrow road toward his ranch.

Brooke unwrapped the foil to find a burrito.

"It's egg and bacon," he told her.

She inhaled the wonderful aroma. "Thank you." How nice that he'd fixed her something to eat. She took one bite, then another. "It's good."

"My specialty." He unwrapped his own sandwich and began to eat as he drove along the bumpy path. He slowed a little. "Sorry, it's a shortcut to the Lucky Bar L."

"I'm fine."

He pointed to the bottle in the cup holder. "There's some orange juice."

She didn't argue, just opened the container and took a big drink of the sweet liquid, then she turned her attention to the man beside her.

The cab was dark, and in the close quarters, she felt a tingling of awareness. There was no denying she was attracted to Trent Landry. She had to fight really hard not to hope for anything more.

She took another drink of her juice, then said, "Thank you for taking me along with you today."

"You might not want to thank me just yet." She heard the amusement in his deep voice. "Let's see how you feel when you get back."

ONCE ON LUCKY Bar L land, Trent continued up the incline until he saw the metal pen he'd used for branding and inoculating his herd over the years. He parked beside the gate, climbed out and watched as Brooke stepped down. He couldn't say what had possessed him to ask her to come along. He cursed under his breath. He knew exactly what had come over him.

Lust.

Over the past months, he'd been spending far too much time out here with only cows to keep him company, or taking men out on hunting and fishing trips. It had been a long time since he had some female companionship.

He glanced at the pretty woman who'd intruded into his solitary life only forty-eight hours ago. Dressed in those snug jeans that covered her perfectly shaped bottom, she made his gut tighten in need. He had to push those thoughts aside. At least until he discovered that she came here for the reason she'd said.

Hearing the sound of horse hooves, he looked up to see Mike and Ricky ride up.

"Hey, Brooke," Ricky called to her as he climbed off his horse.

The other young ranch hand followed behind his friend. "Hi, I'm Mike."

She smiled at him. "Hi, Mike, I'm Brooke Harper."

He put his finger to his hat as he nodded, seeming nervous. "It's nice to meet you, ma'am."

"Please, call me Brooke."

Ricky spoke up. "I hear you're going with us to move the herd."

"Yes, Trent was nice enough to let me come along. I hope I don't slow you down or cause any trouble."

"These two seem to have a knack for that." Trent went around the truck and released the trailer's gate. Again he motioned for Mike's help. The ranch hand walked into the hauler and expertly guided the mare down the ramp.

Trent walked the black horse toward Brooke. He liked how she didn't shy away from the large animal. "Remember Raven? She'll be your mount today."

Brooke reached up and stroked the horse. "Are you sure I can handle her?"

"I have no doubt you can, but I'll be close by if you need help."

"I'll help you, too, Brooke," Ricky chimed in.

Trent took the reins of his mount, Rango, from his ranch hand. "You just worry about getting the herd moved. I'll handle Brooke's safety."

Ricky grinned. "Sure, boss, if you say so."

Returning to Brooke, Trent helped her mount Raven and checked her stirrups. Then he went to his horse, swung his leg over the gelding's back and sat in the saddle. He looked over at Brooke.

"You'll do fine. Just handle the horse like you did yesterday."

He watched as she nodded, then she tugged on the reins and Raven backed away from the pens. Soon, she was taking the mare through commands. He nearly beamed with pride as she got the feel for the animal. She looked damn good on horseback.

"I'd say you're ready to go," he told her.

He dug his heels into Rango, and motioned for Ricky and Mike to head toward the pasture. Trent fell in next to Brooke. Although she seemed to be handling Raven just fine, he wasn't going to stray too far from her. That was his excuse and he was sticking to it.

OVER THE NEXT thirty minutes, the sun made an appearance and they began to warm up. They removed their heavy coats, and Trent showed Brooke how to tie it to her saddle. She had found the ride relaxing, with the gentle sway of the horse. Raven was easy to ride.

Soon Mike called out as the herd came into view just over the rise. "There are about sixty head of mamas and calves," Trent told Brooke. "We had a good winter, and we only lost a few. To protect them, I'll need to inoculate the calves and castrate the males and ship the yearlings to market."

Brooke took time to watch the red and white cows. The new calves were adorable. "They're so cute. How can you sell them off to be slaughtered?"

Trent shifted position in the saddle. "Because it's a business. And there's a big demand for beef."

"We need our hamburgers and steak," she said as she enjoyed the scenery on horseback and the company of the man beside her.

She saw him fighting a smile. "If I remember you weren't complaining last night while you were gnawing on those ribs."

"Guilty. Seeing them grazing in the pasture, it's hard to think they could be my next meal."

"I grew up on a cattle ranch, so it's second nature to me. Being from the city, you probably don't give a thought about where your beef came from."

"I guess Laurel and I really have had different lives."

"It's nice that you have a chance to get to know her. So let me show you how Laurel would ride across the pasture."

"Oh, I don't like the sound of that."

He must have seen her panicked look and reassured her. "Come on, I think you can handle picking up the pace a little. Not too fast, but ease into a canter. Gently dig your heels into Raven's sides."

Brooke did as he asked and the animal started to lengthen its stride. He instructed her how to get into a tempo with the horse.

Grinning, she worked to stay balanced on the mare. She looked at Trent. "How am I doing?"

He looked too satisfied with himself. "Just fine. Now, I want you to learn how to handle sudden turns and stops because Raven is a trained cutting horse. So let her take the lead. If she takes off after a stray, just tug on the reins if you can't handle it."

Brooke found instead of being frightened, she was excited. She wanted to prove to herself and Trent she could do this. She blew out a breath, feeling her heart pound in her chest. After all, she was Rory Quinn's daughter.

Mike and Ricky were waving their arms in the air and shouting to start the herd on its way. There were a lot of complaints from the bovines, bawling and mooing from both mamas and babies.

With Trent's instructions, Mike and Ricky rode to flank the herd, and he and Brooke rode drag beside and behind the cows.

She couldn't stop watching Trent. He looked amazing on his large roan gelding. The way he took charge and sat with such ease. He took off after a wayward calf, and quickly returned, with the little guy running back to his mama.

After another hour, they came upon another small herd, and Ricky and Mike went after them, and shuffled them back into the herd. Even she got to help, when Raven took off after a few cows. Though she was a little frightened at first, it was exhilarating to feel the power of the horse under her.

"Hold on to the horn, Brooke," Trent called to her. "Let the horse do her job."

Brooke followed Trent's instructions and it wasn't long before Raven gathered her lost cows and brought them back to the fold.

Once the cows were on the move at a steady pace, they drove the herd their two-mile trek toward a closer pasture with fresh grass.

TRENT SMILED AS he watched Brooke. She'd done a better job than he thought. In the past two hours, she'd been able to not only stay on her horse but keep the strays close. "Good job, Brooke."

"I didn't help that much, but thanks for letting me come along. It was so much fun."

He was surprised at her excitement. Most women wouldn't enjoy riding drag at the crack of dawn. "You did a lot. You handled Raven almost as if you were an experienced rider."

"Thanks for that, but I have a lot to learn about horses."

"It all takes practice."

She relaxed in the saddle as their horses moved in a slow, steady rhythm behind the herd. "Not sure where I'll be able to use my new talent. I have a feeling in my new position at the hotel, I'll be working a lot of overtime."

"It's a shame you have to stay inside so much." He glanced at the pretty woman beside him, and felt a strange tightness in his chest. "Maybe you'll come back to visit your sister."

When she looked at him, her expression was doubtful. "I'm not sure she even wants me here now."

"You might be surprised. I think Laurel would be thrilled to know she has a sister."

"I'm not so sure. Laurel doesn't even know me, and I'm asking a big favor of her, to come and meet a mother she didn't know existed."

Trent could understand where she was coming from. "I don't see why you think that's your fault. Your mother kept that secret from you, too."

THE RIDE BACK to the barn took another hour, and Brooke enjoyed every minute of it. She knew she'd be sore tomorrow, but this time out in the beautiful country, with Trent, was worth it.

She was acting foolish, letting this Colorado cowboy turn her head, but what would it hurt? A lot if she let herself care.

The years growing up with Coralee, she'd seen her mother make bad choices with men and get hurt sometimes, and often it had been physical abuse. Some of those men were scary, so Brooke knew to stay clear of them. She always found some place to go, like the library, while Coralee was entertaining her gentlemen friends, as she would call them.

Most were anything but gentlemen. More than one of those awful men had tried to come after her. By the time Brooke was a teenager, she'd let her mother know that she'd run away if she brought any more men home.

Coralee's bad luck with men kept Brooke from having a boyfriend, or even dating. Besides, with school and her jobs she'd been too busy to have time for anything else. At twenty-eight, she had zero experience.

She glanced at the handsome Trent astride his large gelding. Her stomach did somersaults. Now she realized what she'd been missing. A big strong man who wanted to be with her, to share things—kisses, problems and an intimate relationship—with. There was that strange feeling in her stomach again. Okay, Trent was out of her league, but maybe she could find a nice guy when she returned to Las Vegas.

Even she got lonely.

LATER THAT DAY, Trent had cleaned up, and dressed in new jeans and a collared shirt for his trip into town. Waiting in the bank lobby, he checked his watch. It was ten after three. He stood and walked to the window. He didn't like to be kept waiting, but he had no choice if he wanted a chance at getting this loan.

He thought about Brooke back at the cabin. When she'd climbed out of the truck after the cattle drive, he could tell she was already getting stiff from the long ride. He was angry with himself for even inviting her to go along. She was a novice rider, if that. But, damn, she was so eager to do well. He could tell yesterday how much she'd enjoyed being on horseback. But two days in a row, and not used to the saddle…he needed to stop and get her some ointment before she got so bad she couldn't walk. He couldn't help thinking about her soaking in a warm tub, then rubbing the cream on her legs and round bottom.

Suddenly he jerked back to the present when his phone signaled he was getting a text.

He punched in to see the message was from Rory. Plan to stay in Denver a little longer. Have you heard any news from the PI?

Trent texted back. Yes, but got limited info. Should hear more in a few days. Not sure how long Brooke can stay.

Trent waited, but there was no response back from Rory. He was about to call the man and find out what was really going on, when the secretary announced that Mr. Parks would see him.

He followed her down the long hall and into an office. Behind the desk was a middle-aged man with thinning hair, wearing wire glasses and a gray business suit. Smiling, the man stood and came around the desk, then held out his hand.

"Mr. Landry. I'm Jason Parks. Please have a seat."

Trent shook his hand. "Call me Trent."

Parks motioned to a large chair and it surprised Trent when the loan officer took the other chair. "I have to say, it's good to finally meet you. I had the pleasure of getting to know your father, Wade." His smile faded. "So sorry for your loss, Trent."

"Thank you." Trent managed to get the words out of his tight throat.

Parks chuckled. "I have to say that Wade 'Wild-ride' Landry was quite a character." The man's hazel gaze locked on his. "He sure talked about you a lot."

"He did?" Trent asked, sounding more surprised than he wanted to.

"Yes, he was proud of his son in Special Forces. Of course, he got so worried when you were deployed so many times, but that's to be expected when a son goes off to war."

Trent felt uncomfortable talking about the man he hadn't seen or known in years. It was a shame that a stranger had talked with his dad more than his own son.

Jason Parks brought him out of his thoughts. "We could probably swap stories about Wade all day, but I'm sure you didn't come here for that. What can I do for you, Trent?"

Good, back to business. "I need a construction loan to finish my building project." He pulled a paper from his pocket, outlining his goals and everything he needed to finish the cabins. And of course, the amount he needed to borrow. He'd been up late last night coming up with the amount. "I have money in a retirement fund and substantial savings that I'd like to use for collateral."

Jason walked around his desk as he looked over the proposal. "Why not use the Lucky Bar L?"

"I don't want to risk the ranch." He leaned forward.

"Look, Jason. You had to hear about our contractor running off with the money Rory Quinn and I had for the project."

At the man's nod, Trent continued, "Well, I plan to finish the cabins myself. I'll be the general contractor this time, and hire all the trades to do the work. If you can't help me out, I'll go look elsewhere, because the buildings need to be completed before the first snow."

Jason Parks nodded. "Then I guess we need to get down to business and figure this out."

Chapter Eight

That evening in her cabin, Brooke groaned as she shifted
her aching body into a deeper, more comfortable position
in the oversize bathtub. Nothing seemed to help ease the
pain. After Trent dropped her off from their ride earlier,
she'd only managed to fall into bed for a nap, but it hadn't
helped the stiffness in her legs and bottom.

Who would have thought riding a horse could hurt
so much? Although she was proud of the fact she hadn't
fallen off Raven, and she had the satisfaction of helping
Trent move the herd.

Brooke laid her head on the rolled towel she'd placed at
the edge of the tub. She closed her eyes and her thoughts
automatically turned to the cowboy she'd gotten to see in
action this morning.

Not only had Trent looked commanding astride his
horse, she'd also gotten to see a gentler side of the man
when he'd freed a small calf tangled in some fencing. The
sight of him cradling the tiny bovine in those big strong
arms was so heartwarming, and after hearing the phrase *a
total turn-on* several times, she now knew what it meant.

A warm feeling stirred her body. What woman could
resist that? If she let herself, she could easily take the tumble. But she couldn't keep dreaming up fantasies about
this man.

She needed to remember she had a mother who was in a care facility, with Alzheimer's, and her dream job still wasn't hers yet. Then there was a twin sister and a father she never knew about. And there was a good chance that Rory and Laurel would reject her. Her chest tightened with the familiar ache.

Doubt set in again. Oh, God. What was she doing here, going horseback riding and sleeping in a fancy cabin that belonged to a family that would never be hers? She shouldn't be wasting time thinking about a man just because he gave her a little attention. Trent Landry was out of her league. She had no idea how to play the male-female games. And what would he do when he learned the entire truth about her?

Seeing her fingers begin to shrivel like a prune, Brooke started to get out of the tub, but her sore muscles rebelled and she leaned back with another groan, and turned on the soothing jets.

She closed her eyes and sank deeper into the tub as the bubbles covered her breasts in a warm caress. The picture of the sexy cowboy with the deep-set chocolate eyes and a cleft chin flashed back into her head. Ten more minutes for a fantasy wasn't going hurt.

TRENT WALKED UP on the cabin porch, balancing food containers in one hand so he could knock on the door. He waited a few seconds but there was no answer, not even a sound from inside. Where was Brooke? He glanced at her compact car parked beside his truck. It was already dark so he hoped she wasn't running around outside on her own.

He tried the knob and it was locked. Good.

"Brooke?" he called but was met with silence again. Worried, he used the master key and opened the door, then walked into the empty room. "Brooke? It's Trent. Are you here?"

He set the bags of food on the table and made his way down the hall, calling Brooke's name so as to not startle her. He glanced inside the one bedroom to find the bed hadn't been made. Then he saw clothes on the floor, the jeans and blouse Brooke had worn that morning. He stopped short seeing her lacy pink panties and bra. Thoughts of a naked Brooke flashed through his head. When his body reacted, he swiftly shook the picture away. He needed to find her.

Trent continued his search and headed to the last room in the small cabin, the bath. He hesitated as he reached the open door, knowing he should give Brooke privacy. He also needed to see that she was okay. At least that was what he told himself.

He nearly stumbled when he saw her lying in the tub. Her eyes were closed, and her lips slightly parted, letting him know she was sound asleep. His gaze moved down to her body, thanking the Lord that the soapy water kept her modesty intact. Barely. Even that didn't make any difference to his suddenly active libido. He sucked air into his starved lungs. *Okay, get a grip, Landry. What are you, fifteen?*

A moan came from the tub, and his pulse shot off. He quietly jerked the door partly shut but the view of a naked Brooke had been burned into his brain.

He leaned against the wall, working to pull himself together. Maybe he should just leave. No. It wasn't safe; she was in a tub.

Taking a relaxing breath, he raised his fist and began to knock on the door. "Brooke! Brooke, are you in there?"

Not a sound. He knocked hard. "Brooke. It's Trent. If you don't answer, I'm coming in there."

He waited a few more seconds, then he heard her voice. "Trent? What are you doing here?"

With the sound of water splashing he knew she was climbing out of the tub. Naked.

He shut his eyes, and damn, if he couldn't imagine water sluicing down her slim body, her full breasts, along the curve of those hips. He swallowed and managed to say, "I brought you some…ointment for your sore muscles."

There was a pause, then the door opened a crack and her face appeared, damp curls circling her face. She looked adorable and sexy as hell. He glanced down to see that she was wrapped in a towel. "And some supper," he managed.

Her eyes went wide in surprise, as if she, too, recognized the intimacy of the situation. "I'll be out in a few minutes."

He jerked his thumb in the direction of the hall. "I'll… just go back to the living room. Holler if you need anything." He turned and walked down the hall before he did something stupid.

FIFTEEN MINUTES LATER, Brooke finally made an appearance. It had taken her that long to get the nerve up to face Trent. She knew that the bathroom door had been open when she'd gotten into the tub. A shiver went through her knowing he had to have seen her. He had done the gentlemanly thing, closed the door before he'd called out to her.

She'd put on a pair of sweats and socks, leaving her hair in a loose ponytail and walked into the living room. She stopped short and her pulse shot up a notch when she got a load of the man waiting for her. Minus his cowboy hat, his thick brown hair lay in waves across his high forehead. His chiseled jaw showed off the fact that he had shaved recently. He was dressed in a light blue collared shirt and black jeans.

"Hi…"

He smiled. "Do you feel better?"

"Much," she said, as heat crawled up her neck then to her face. She worked to keep her movements slow and even. "The bath helped a lot."

He held up the paper bag. "This might help, too. Some call it a magic ointment."

She reached inside and took out a bottle of ibuprofen, then a large jar of cream. She read the label. "This says it's for animals."

He shrugged. "All I know is it works great on sore muscles. I've used it myself many times, especially when I first came back to the ranch. I hadn't ridden in years." He motioned with his hand. "Go put some on and I'll warm up some dinner."

"I should help you," she said.

"I can handle this." Trent folded his arms across his chest. Even in pain, dressed in baggy sweats, and her hair pulled into a messy ponytail, she was damn appealing.

She straightened. "Stop trying to intimidate me, Mr. Sergeant Major."

And feisty. "Look, I'm the one who let you sit in the saddle most of the day. Humor me, Brooke, and try the cream. And also take some ibuprofen."

She glared back, then finally relented and turned and walked away.

It killed Trent to see her wince in pain. At least she'd soaked in the tub. That should help her some.

Suddenly a picture of her rubbing the cream over her body popped into his mind, but he quickly shook it away. "Get a grip."

Busying himself with supper, he set place mats on the

coffee table, along with paper plates and plastic forks. He knew Brooke would be more comfortable on the sofa.

Tasks completed, he stood back and eyed the makeshift table. He thought about lighting candles, then stopped himself. This wasn't a seduction, just a simple meal with a visitor to the ranch. Off in the distance, he heard the rumble of thunder. A storm was moving through tonight, promising some much-needed rain. Those candles might be needed after all.

Trent went back to the counter and opened two foil-wrapped containers from the diner in town and placed them in the preheated oven to keep warm.

Ten minutes later, Brooke came out of the bathroom. Moving slowly, she made her way into the room, and smiled as she looked around.

"Oh, Trent. What have you done?"

Her soft, husky voice caused his body to react again. He took the containers out. "If you have to ask, then I guess I did it wrong."

"No, that's not what I meant. You didn't need to do all this."

"It's only Monday night's meat-loaf special from the diner." He shrugged. "Since I was in town, anyway, I thought I'd bring back supper, especially since I knew you'd be a little sore from today's ride."

She seemed to relax at his comments. "And I thank you for going to all this trouble. You're spoiling me, and I'm not used to… I mean, I don't get the chance to enjoy many evening meals."

He escorted her to the sofa, wondering about the kind of men who'd been in her life. "Well, you're getting spoiled tonight."

She sank down onto the leather sofa. "You're not going to want to sit too close—the smell is pretty strong." She

wrinkled her cute nose. "The ointment is wicked. I slath-
ered on a pretty good dose."

Smiling, he couldn't help imagining her hands working
the cream over her long slender legs. "Give it a few hours
and you'll see it's worth the odor." He needed to concentrate on something else. Supper. "I poured you water, but
if you want something else…"

"No, this is fine."

Trent dished the food onto the plates, then carried them
to the table.

"Oh, this looks wonderful." Brooke started to scoot
forward, but he stopped her.

"Let me make it easier for you." He reached under the
coffee table, released the latch and pulled the top up, making it table height.

She smiled. "How nice."

That pleased look caused his pulse to race. "Rory and I
decided our guests should be able to enjoy a game on the
television." He nodded toward the bare wall and sat down
next to her. "Soon there'll be a large flat screen hanging
there. They'll have a front-row seat right here."

She bit off a piece of the roll. "Are you going ahead
with the building?"

Nodding, he swallowed a bite of meat loaf. "There isn't
any choice, unless we both want to lose our investment.
Earlier today, I went to the bank to work out a loan. I've
been approved, and I've already hired a carpenter, a roofer
and a plumber. If this rainstorm moves through tonight,
the rest of the week looks clear to begin the work."

A rumble of thunder filled the silence as she picked up
her fork. "What about Rory?"

"He texted me today and let me know he'll be home in
a few days. He has other things on his mind, and he hasn't
texted me back about the loan. I had to go ahead with this.

Winter is coming, along with snow, and any more delays could cause us more trouble." He looked at her. "Are you still able to stay until Laurel and the family get back?"

She shrugged. "Like I said before, I've taken some vacation time for the week. But if I hear from the Dream Chaser Hotel about me being hired, I'll have to leave."

Four days. That excited him more than it should. "You don't sound happy about it."

"I'm worried about my mother. Erin, at the care facility, has assured me that she's been doing well. Of course, Coralee is anxious for me to talk with Laurel."

"I'm sorry," he said. "You have a lot of things you put on hold waiting until the Quinns come home. Funny thing is, Rory usually never leaves the ranch. Diane has always had to drag him away for even a short vacation."

Brooke shrugged. "I did show up here unannounced."

She enjoyed talking to Trent. He was a good listener. Most men she had known wanted to talk about themselves, and none had been as interesting as Trent. Okay, none were as good-looking either.

She took a bite of her mashed potatoes and the buttery favor had her closing her eyes. "Oh, my gosh. These are delicious."

"Bill's specialty. And his meat loaf, too."

Ten minutes later, their plates were empty, and everything had been eaten.

"Well, that was shameful." Brooke sank back onto the sofa. "I can't believe I ate all that food."

Trent nodded. "Horseback riding is great exercise. You burned a lot of calories today."

"And I think I'm crippled for life," she joked.

He frowned. "That's my fault. I never should have let you ride two days in a row."

"I'm glad you did, because I'll probably never have the chance again. So thank you for such a wonderful day."

AN HOUR LATER, Trent glanced down at Brooke's peaceful face. She had somehow positioned herself against him. One minute they'd been sitting comfortably on the sofa, just talking about Laurel and Rory. Then he'd noticed her lack of conversation and looked at her. She was sound asleep.

He would laugh about the situation if his body hadn't been in a constant state of arousal since she'd snuggled up to him. There was nothing he wanted more than to kiss her sweet mouth, and feel her body under his while he made love to her. He dropped his head back on the sofa with a groan. He began to visualize several more fantasies with one pretty blonde. And none of them were G-rated.

Brooke shifted in her sleep and her hand moved dangerously close to the waistband of his jeans.

He couldn't take much more.

As carefully as possible, he held her away from him as he stood, then he leaned down and lifted her into his arms.

Brooke stirred and opened her eyes. "Trent…"

His heart pounded in his chest, hearing her whisper his name. "That's right, babe, I'm here." He started walking down the hall and into her dark room. "It's time for you to be in bed."

"Oh, okay. So tired."

He couldn't believe how trusting she was with him. Reluctant to let her go, he managed to place her down on the mattress, then he pulled a blanket and quilt over her. He felt her shiver and he reached for another blanket off the chair, and layered it on top of the quilt.

A flash of lightning shone across Brooke's face as she turned on her side, then snuggled into the pillow. Crouching down beside the bed, Trent brushed the hair from her face. He felt something tighten around his heart as he watched her sleep. Unable to resist any longer, he leaned closer and placed a gentle kiss against her cheek. "Good night, cowgirl."

Brooke's eyes blinked open. "You kissed me."

He couldn't help a smile. "Just a good-night kiss."

Suddenly a strange expression crossed her face. "No one ever kisses me." Then her eyes drifted shut and soon he heard the soft sound of her breathing, letting him know she'd fallen asleep again.

He stood and walked out of the room. Nobody ever kissed her? What did that mean? No men? Not her mother?

Trent carried their paper plates into the kitchen and dumped them in the trash can under the sink. He thought back to his own childhood, his brother's death, then his parents' divorce and the lonely years in the military. He'd found he still wanted to come back here to the Lucky Bar L. Maybe find what he'd lost, exorcise ghosts from the past.

He thought about the woman in the next room. He fought the urge to go back and pull Brooke into his arms and hold her. Something told him she hadn't had much of that in her life. Whether or not she had, he couldn't let her get close. Brooke Harper was still a mystery to him and he might need help to figure her out.

He grabbed a towel to wipe off his hands, then grabbed his jacket and headed out the door. *Rory Quinn, you need to get home and take care of business.* He walked out into the storm, but it was nothing compared to the one brewing inside him.

Chapter Nine

The next morning, the sun was up and the sky, clear. Trent looked out his cabin window as he sipped his third cup of coffee. He'd been up for two hours, helped the men feed the barn stock, and been on the phone with Ricky to check on the Lucky Bar L. They'd been fortunate the storm had passed through the area, and hadn't done any damage.

He couldn't help wondering about Brooke. Did she awake during the night scared? He suspected the Las Vegas desert had its fair share of storms, but in Colorado, at a higher elevation, the thunderclaps were a lot louder.

Okay, he was getting far too drawn to this woman. That could be bad news, especially if Brooke developed a relationship with the Quinns. Worse, if she didn't. And there was Rory and his past association with Coralee Harper. From what he sensed by the anger in Rory's voice the last time they talked on the phone, it hadn't been a good one. How would that affect Brooke? Would Rory resent her, too?

Trent shook his head. He still couldn't get his head around the fact Laurel wasn't Diane's biological daughter. Now Laurel had a sister, too, but would she welcome Brooke?

He wasn't sure about any of this. He didn't want to

choose sides, either. How could he go against his friend, if Rory didn't want Brooke around?

He shut his eyes. Three days ago, he didn't know Brooke Harper. Now, she was stirring up things he hadn't let himself feel in a long time. He couldn't let it matter, because she'd be gone by the end of the week.

He only hoped she would at least be able to make a connection with Laurel. Everyone needed a family. He absently rubbed his chest, feeling the familiar tightness. It wasn't fair that the sisters had to suffer for their mother's sins.

Suddenly his phone rang and he reached for it on the counter. It was Brooke. He pressed the button and said, "Good morning."

"Good morning to you, too," she said, then there was a pause before she added, "Sorry for falling asleep last night."

"Not a problem. You were tired."

"But you carried me to bed."

"So you remembered," he challenged, knowing he hadn't forgotten cradling her slight body in his arms.

"Not exactly… I mean not everything, but since you were the only person here, I'm pretty sure you were the one. I hope I didn't embarrass myself."

"Not at all. Besides I'm the one who wore you out, getting you up at dawn and putting you on a horse all day."

"Oh, my, it was so terrible," she dramatized. "You forced me at gunpoint and threatened me."

He was grinning like a stupid teenager. "Well, you get today off. So relax, you've earned it."

"Are you going out with the herd?"

"No, I'm meeting with some of the construction crew a little later."

"How about right now?" she asked. "Are you busy now?"

"No. Why?"

"Why don't you answer your door and find out."

He walked across the room, finding he was getting excited about seeing her. He pulled open the door to find her standing there with two covered plates. "Special delivery."

"Hello, sunshine."

She blushed as she walked inside. "You've been feeding me so often, I thought I would return the favor."

He inhaled the wonderful aroma of bacon and eggs. "There's no need, but I'm not going to turn you away."

She smiled shyly. "I wasn't sure what you liked, but I only had a few things in the cabin refrigerator. So I made scrambled eggs with bacon and some home fries."

Mouth watering, he took the plates from her and walked to the counter since it was the only table in the cabin.

She hadn't followed him. "Oh, Trent. You have no furniture." She glanced around the empty room. "What are you sleeping on?" She took off down the hall before he could stop her. When she returned, she was frowning. "You can't sleep on a blow-up mattress."

He took her hand and felt a strange zing shoot up his arm. "First of all, you aren't letting me do anything. I made the decision to stay here."

She raised those big green eyes to meet his. "But…"

"Listen, this place is a five-star hotel compared to some of the accommodations I had while deployed. If I got any sleep at all. That bed in there is pretty comfortable."

She released a sigh. "I still don't like it. I'm fine staying out here by myself. You can go back to your ranch and sleep in your own bed."

"I know, but for now, this is fine." He grinned. "Although, I love having someone make me breakfast." He took the foil off the plates and his mouth began to water at the pile of scrambled eggs with diced bacon and fried potatoes. "Woman, if you cook like this, you're never going to get rid of me."

Brooke felt the heat climb up her cheeks. She hadn't been sure if Trent would appreciate her just barging in this morning. He had a lot more things to do than babysit her. And she would make sure she stayed out of his hair today. Maybe she could go into town and look around, or read a book, or go catch up with her emails. Call the Dream Chaser Hotel to see if there was any news. None of those things interested her as much as making breakfast for Trent.

She was in big trouble.

Trent reached behind the counter and grabbed a bottle of water. "I don't have anything to drink beside water and coffee," he told her.

She nodded. "Coffee is fine."

He had an extra mug and poured the aromatic brew. "Sorry, no cream or sugar."

"That's fine, I take it black. And the stronger the better."

"A woman after my own heart."

"I spent a lot of time studying. I needed something to help keep me awake."

He carried the full mug to the counter. "That's quite an accomplishment, working full-time and going to college. Your mother has to be proud of you."

She tensed. Coralee had never understood her need for an education. She'd hated that Brooke was away so much. "Yes, my getting a better job is important for her care."

He picked up a fork, dug into the eggs and took a bite. "Wow, this is so good."

She loved watching his expression. "It's just eggs with some chopped-up bacon in it."

"And made with loving care, as my mother used to say."

A pang of envy struck her. "Are you and your mother close?"

He nodded. "We stay in touch mostly with phone calls, but I haven't made it back to Denver in about a year." He shrugged. "She's happy with her life there, and also that I came back to take over the ranch."

Brooke swallowed her eggs. "Maybe she'll come here for a visit."

When she saw a sad look transform Trent's face, she quickly realized her mistake. "Oh, Trent, I'm sorry, I shouldn't have said, I mean… Of course, she wouldn't want to come back to the home of her ex-husband."

"No, Brooke, Mom had bad memories before the divorce. They're of Chris from when he died here."

She groaned. "Sorry, I wasn't thinking…"

Trent reached out and took her hand. "It's okay, Brooke. I know you didn't mean anything by it. Those memories are hard for all of us."

She wanted to ask him about the tragedy that took his brother away, but knew he might not want to share with her.

He turned back to his food and began eating again. Brooke did the same, but she couldn't stop thinking about the man who let her see glimpses of his pain. His parents hadn't been the only ones who suffered over a young boy's death.

Once finished, Trent carried his plate to the sink. "Do you have plans for today?"

"Maybe a drive into town. Why, do you need me to bring you back anything?"

He leaned against the sink, and crossed his booted feet. "Now that's an offer I can't refuse. I've called in an order at the lumberyard, but I can't get it delivered until tomorrow. And I need to be here to start the crew working. Could you pick it up?"

"Of course, but my compact isn't very large."

He frowned. "That's why you'll take my truck." He reached into his pocket, pulled out his keys and tossed them to her.

She grabbed them out of the air. He trusted her with his truck? "Just give me the directions."

"I have a GPS."

"Okay, then, I'll go, but you're doing the dishes."

She heard his laughter as she walked out the door. She may only be here a few days, so why not have a good time?

THE TOWN OF Hidden Springs had a population of only a little more than nine thousand residents. In the summer, people came from all over to ride the rapids on the Colorado River. In the winter, they came for the ideal skiing conditions.

With the help of the GPS, she found the lumberyard easily. She got a friendly greeting, and the employees were eager to load Trent's order. One man there looked at her twice, but didn't say anything. He smiled a lot and gave her a wink as she drove off. Probably thought she was Laurel.

Brooke couldn't help wondering how nice it would have been to grow up here. To have a permanent home and parents who loved her and supported her.

Windows down, country-and-western music playing on the radio, Brooke drove the oversize truck along the highway and headed back to the ranch. She couldn't live on fantasies. Her life was back in Las Vegas, with a mother in a nursing home, and she was the only one available to take care of her.

There was no time to dream about a life that would

never be hers. She had to live in the real world. But for a little while she was going to enjoy this time. She raised the volume on the radio and sang along to the song.

Ten minutes later, she turned off at her exit, then took the road to the Bucking Q and felt her excitement grow knowing she was going to spend some time with Trent.

She drove by the Quinns' big home, then past the finished cabins and headed to the construction site. Parking the truck, she killed the engine and climbed out. Immediately, Trent appeared and walked toward her. He'd replaced his cowboy hat for a hard hat.

He smiled. "That was fast," he said and handed her a hat. "Here, put this on. It's a rule on job sites."

She slipped the hard plastic hat on her head. "I would have been waiting longer, but this nice man, Johnny Mattson, hurried over and began filling the order."

Trent laughed. "Sounds like Johnny. Just send him a pretty woman and he knocks himself out to impress her. He didn't bother you, did he?"

"No. He was just being friendly. He asked if I was related to Laurel."

Trent arched an eyebrow. "What did you tell him?"

"I just said maybe."

Trent laughed again and it made her insides tingle. "Good job." He walked to the back of the truck and pulled down the tailgate. He waved at two men and they began unloading the lumber.

Feeling that she was in the way, Brooke said, "If you don't need me to do anything else, I'll just head back to the cabin."

"Hey, don't leave. I want to show you around." He shrugged. "Unless you don't want to see what's going on."

Her pulse raced with excitement. "I'd love to see what

you're doing." She nodded at the largest structure. "What is that building going to be?"

"That's the Q and L Guest Lodge. Come on, I'll show you inside."

Surprising her, he took hold of her hand. She let him walk her across the rain-soaked earth for a closer look. Good thing she had on Laurel's boots.

The two-story building had been framed, log walls had been sealed and the green metal roof was on. She heard the buzz of the saws and the pop of the nail guns in the background.

"It's starting to take shape, but there's still a lot to do. There were so many delays even when Aldrich was the contractor. So many things he said he'd done but hadn't. Now I know why. He'd taken the money for himself and we couldn't pay the vendors."

Trent waved his hand, as if he didn't want to discuss the man any longer. "My expectations are more realistic now. I'm shooting for the outside structure to be completed before next month. We're nearly in October and we could get snow any time."

She shivered, aware of the drop in temperature after last night's storm. She only had on a thin jacket. "Is it possible to get snow now?"

He nodded. "That's why we need to get the doors and windows we ordered. Maybe I should send you to the window guy. You seem to have a knack for getting things done."

If he didn't quit smiling at her like that, she'd melt on the spot. "I'll help if you want. I'm used to supervising." She prided herself on handling many situations. She hoped it was enough to get her hired at Dream Chaser.

"I was thinking I might have some suggestions for help on the inside."

Trent called out instructions to one of the crew, then he came back to her and took her up the steps to a large porch and inside the building. The scent of fresh-cut wood filled her and she inhaled deeply. "Oh, it smells so good in here."

He grinned at her. "I agree."

Again she felt the strange tingling. She turned her attention to a great room that took up most of the first floor. There were the beginnings of an open staircase that was against the wall, climbing to the second floor. A stacked-stone fireplace took up most of another wall; the final wall was all windows, facing the glorious view of the mountain. At least, it would be windows when glass got put in. Now, the openings were covered in heavy plastic.

"This will be amazing when it's finished. How many bedrooms?"

"There's six," he told her. "We're planning to install an industrial, stainless-steel kitchen in back, hoping to rent the place out for big fishing parties, maybe family reunions and business retreats."

"Wow, you aren't messing around. I'm jealous. You'll be able to get up close and personal with your guests. I can't do that in a large Las Vegas hotel."

"But we'll never be able to compete with a name-brand hotel. The only amenities we can offer might be a continental breakfast and some Western barbecue."

"Great idea. Work out a deal with Joe's Smoke House to use his barbecue sauce and sell it right here." She walked to a makeshift table covered in building plans. "At the front desk."

Trent blinked at her, as if she spoke a foreign language. Okay, maybe she'd gone too far. "Sorry, I get a little carried away sometimes."

"No, it's okay. It's just we hadn't thought much past the furnished building, and me being the fishing and hunting outfitter. That's how this idea for the cabins first came into play. The sportsmen wanted to stay closer than in town at a motel."

"And you're going to make good money with just renting the cabins to the hunters and fishermen."

He stood back and gave her that stern look she'd gotten used to, but still wasn't sure what it meant. "What else do you think we could do with this place?"

She couldn't keep her excitement contained any longer as she raised her hands in a sweeping motion. "Since you have all this land, you could rent the building out for small weddings. Even team up with caterers and florists from town."

"You seem to know a lot about this."

"I might be a card dealer, but while in college I interned at the Dream Chaser Hotel and their main business is weddings."

"But you're Las Vegas—we're small-town."

"There's a lot of competition there, too. You have to offer the client something special."

"Weddings seem to be a lot of work."

"Then just advertise the building for weddings inside, and land outside, too. Let the couple hire an event planner to do all the work. Just saying that you're not always in the hunting season, but you're always in wedding season."

Suddenly, Trent gave her a teasing wink. "Hell, woman, I'm only trying to build hunting and fishing cabins and now you've got me thinking about weddings."

Chapter Ten

Deep down, Brooke knew Trent was teasing, but darn, it didn't stop the heat from creeping up her neck and face.

She couldn't let him get to her. Keep the situation light. "You seem to have an aversion to marriage, Mr. Landry?"

"Damn straight." He tossed her a wicked grin. "The only commitment I ever had was to the army, and that came to an end a while back."

Suddenly she wanted to know more about his personal life. "You're saying you never had a special girl in your life who made you think about marriage?"

"Maybe in my early years. But being career military, I couldn't see leaving a woman home while I was off on a mission. Sometimes I was gone for months at a time." He leaned against the worktable and studied her. "What about you, Miss Harper? Have you ever come close to marriage?"

She shook her head. "When would I have had time?"

His intense gaze combed over her. "Come on, a pretty girl like you, the boys probably flocked to you."

He thought she was pretty.

"Since Laurel was fifteen, she's had all kinds of guys sniffing around her. Rory had a rough time. Good thing he had a shotgun ready."

A pang of envy hit her in the chest. "Were you one of them?" Oh, God, had she just said that?

There was the wicked grin again. "She was like a kid sister to me. But I helped weed out the bad guys."

How nice it would have been to have someone watch over her.

He continued to study her. "You still haven't answered my question. Anyone special?"

She shook her head. "I was more the studious type and had a part-time job after school so I couldn't do social activities."

Trent's gaze zeroed in on hers. "I'm kind of glad those boys stayed away."

Her heart raced off. "Why is that?"

"I used to be one of those teenage boys, so I know what they wanted, and it wasn't a nice girl."

"Sounds like you still don't want a nice girl."

"I'm well past wanting girls, I want—"

The sound of his cell phone interrupted his thought. "Excuse me," he told her and answered it. He turned away as he talked. She glanced around the large structure. She would love to see it finished, but that wouldn't happen.

She should head back to the cabin, but why? She had nothing to do there. Okay, she could go into town again, take her laundry, or play tourist for a while.

Trent said her name and she turned around.

"That was Ricky. Red Baron got his leg caught in some fencing."

"Oh, no. Is he okay?"

"Not sure. I need to get to the ranch."

"Of course. Go."

"Would you go with me?" he asked as he waved for one of the crew.

"You don't have to take me, Trent. I'm fine here."

He didn't look happy. "I need to get to the ranch, to meet the vet. Do you want to go with me or not?"

"Yes, I want to go."

"Then let's go." He escorted her to the truck and helped her into her seat. He walked around the hood and called to one of the workers.

Common sense told her to stay away from Trent, but she didn't care. Even if she told herself she was tagging along because she was concerned about the injured horse, she knew the truth. It was the man she wanted to spend time with.

Two HOURS LATER in the barn at the Lucky Bar L, Trent stood in the large stall. Red Baron lay on the straw floor sedated, while the vet stitched up the long gash in his front leg.

He'd calmed somewhat over the stallion's accident. He glanced at Brooke as she leaned over the railing watching everything going on. She'd been the cool one reminding him that his horse would be fine. He wanted to rip into Ricky for not being more careful with the valuable animal.

He glanced at her. And she gave him a smile that caused a funny feeling in his chest.

The large horse blew out a breath, letting everyone know the medication was wearing off.

The young vet, Matt Carpenter, quickly bandaged the leg, then stood. "Good thing I'm finished," he said, stripping off his rubber gloves. He gave Trent an encouraging smile. "Red will be sporting about a ten-inch scar, but the X-ray shows no tendon damage. He should be fine to ride again, just hold off a few weeks. I'll check him again in a week."

Trent nodded, finally breathing easier as Red raised his head and blew out another loud breath. He rubbed the animal's muzzle. "It's okay, boy." He thought his dream of breeding this magnificent horse might have ended today.

Trent stood and shook the vet's hand. "I can't thank you enough, Matt."

"No problem, Trent. I like it when my day turns out this way." The man shook his head. "I'd hate to have to put down any animal, but this guy is special."

"I know."

The vet looked at Brooke. "It was nice to meet you, too, Brooke. I hope I'll see you again before you leave town."

"Nice meeting you, too."

Trent saw her uneasiness. The Quinns should be home tomorrow and he couldn't help wondering how that was going to play out. But right now, his concern was his horse. Before the vet left, they both helped the stallion to his feet. Once Matt saw the horse hadn't had any aftereffects to the drug, he bade goodbye and left.

Brooke watched as Trent went back into the stall and wrapped his arms around the stallion's neck and hugged him close. The touching scene stole her heart. The big, tough army sergeant was showing his softer side.

Trent finally released his hold on the animal and looked at her. "I'm sorry this has taken so long."

"I'm not complaining, Trent." At the sound of her voice, Red came to the railing and she reached out. "You're worth it, big guy, aren't you?" She felt honored that the horse allowed her to pet him. "I'm just happy that you're okay."

"Damn, it's nearly six o'clock. Come on, let's go up to the house and see if there's anything to eat."

He came out of the stall and went to help her down. "Only if you let me fix it," she told him. "You've been bringing me food for the past three days."

"It's not a problem, but I'm not going to turn you down if you want to cook for me."

"Hope you're not sorry. I'm not that good."

The sound of his laughter echoed through the barn and outside. With the setting sun, there was a sudden drop in temperature. She crossed her arms to keep warm.

"Cold?"

With her nod, he placed his arm across her shoulders and pulled her close. "When we get to the house, I'll make a fire."

The picture of them snuggled together in front of a blazing fire had her warming all over.

He walked her up the steps, then released her and opened the door, allowing her inside ahead of him.

Even though she'd only seen the old-style kitchen, she was quickly falling in love with the house. Surprising her, he walked her into the next room, a dining room, with a dark mahogany table with six high-back chairs. He continued on until they reached a large living room with an open beam ceiling. The floors were gleaming hardwood, partly covered with Berber rugs. Two leather sofas were arranged in front of the floor-to-ceiling brick fireplace. A rough-cut log served as the mantel and above it was a huge flat-screen television.

"Wow! That's quite a television."

He shrugged. "What can I say? When I have the time, I like to watch sports." He changed the subject. "I have some steaks in the freezer, how about I barbecue a couple?"

"Hey, I thought I was cooking for you."

"You are. You can microwave potatoes and find a vegetable."

"Sounds good," she said as she glanced around. "May I use your bathroom?"

"Of course," he said, and pointed down the hall. "Second door on the left."

She started off past the staircase leading to the second floor. Was that where Trent slept? She shook away any thoughts about the man in bed. Opening the door to the old-fashioned bathroom, she smiled at the peach-colored tiles along the counter and in the large tub area. After using the facilities, she washed her hands and started back to the kitchen. In the long hall, she spotted a row of old photos hanging on the wall.

The first ones were older pictures of a man holding a large belt buckle. All-around cowboy. He looked so much like Trent it had to be his father, Wade Landry. The next picture was another one of Wade Landry, standing beside another man at a rodeo, big smiles on their faces. The second man was about the same height and build as Wade, but he had lighter coloring and auburn curly hair under his cowboy hat. Had to be Rory Quinn. Her father.

She released a breath. She'd seen Rory's picture before. She'd Googled his name once she'd learned who he was, but seeing him on a family picture wall made it seem so real.

"That was taken at National Finals Rodeo nineteen eighty-seven."

Brooke jumped and turned to see Trent. "Sorry." Her heart raced, feeling as if she'd been caught stealing. "I was just… I mean, that's your dad, right?"

Trent nodded as he came closer. "That was the year they won the national finals in team roping. Rory also won the All-Around Cowboy title." He stood so close to her, she could feel his heat, smell his now familiar scent. "I was a baby back then."

"Do you remember that day?"

He shook his head. "My mother said I saw part of it, but that last day, I was back at the hotel with a babysitter."

Brooke couldn't help wondering if Coralee was at the

rodeo. Had Rory taken her to the event? She wanted to know about their relationship. Had he at least cared something for her mother? Or was she just there to warm his bed?

"Are you thinking about your mother with Rory?"

She turned to him. "What?"

"If you count back to that year, that had to be the weekend that Rory met Coralee, and Laurel was conceived."

Tell him the truth. She turned back to the pictures to see school pictures of two young boys. The older boy was about ten years old and had short brown hair and deepset eyes. She smiled. Even back then, Trent Landry was a serious child.

"You were cute."

"I'm not anymore?" he teased.

She laughed and turned her attention back to the pictures and the other boy. He looked to be about six or seven with a freckled face, lighter hair and a big smile.

"That's Christopher," Trent said.

Her heart squeezed, hearing the pain in Trent's voice. "How old was he here?"

"Seven." There was a long pause. "He died when he was nine." He pointed to another picture. "That's his last school picture."

Brooke couldn't stop herself. She wrapped her arms around his waist and pressed her face against his chest, then asked, "How did he die?"

"He was riding his horse, Buckeye, and trying to catch up with me when he fell off and went down into a ravine." She felt his hands tighten across her back and pull her closer. "He wasn't found until nightfall."

She heard the thumping of his heart under her ear. Of course the pain was still there. "I'm so sorry, Trent."

He breathed out a sigh. "So am I. Chris deserved a better brother."

She pulled back and looked up into his face. His gaze met hers, but neither of them spoke. All she knew was the joy she felt having Trent hold her. But the feeling was quickly turning into something more. He felt it, too. Their eyes met, then he lowered his head, and brushed his mouth across hers.

Brooke sucked in a breath as her lips parted and his mouth covered hers, tasting, teasing. She was practically begging for more.

He pulled back, looking down at her. "Open for me, Brooke."

She shivered and did as he asked, then his mouth came down in total possession, hard and insistent. He pushed his tongue deep inside.

She moaned at the sheer pleasure, and pleaded for more, wanting to ease the tension growing in her. His arms tightened around her and she pressed her breasts against the hard wall of his chest.

It was Trent who groaned this time. Brooke's mouth was soft and warm and so tempting. He lifted his mouth and searched her wide eyes. His gaze moved to her swollen lips. He ached to dive back in and forget about everything except burying himself in her body, and erase all the pain and loneliness in his life. Not a good idea right now. There were too many unanswered questions. But damn, she tempted him.

Instead, he pressed his forehead against hers, but didn't want to release her just yet. "You are one helluva sexy lady, Brooke Harper, but I think it would be safer if we go into the kitchen and eat some supper."

She nodded against his chest. He cupped her chin and

made her look at him. "Hey, I'm trying to be a gentleman here."

She didn't meet his eyes. "You're right, food sounds good." She broke the hold, then walked off down the hall. Trent watched the sway of her jeans-covered bottom and cursed his decision.

AN HOUR LATER, Brooke pushed her plate away, with a half-eaten steak still adorning it.

"I can't eat another bite," she said. "I'm stuffed."

Trent smiled. "Come on, I watched you put away those ribs the other night. You can do better than that."

"Yes, but I didn't have a big baked potato and vegetables to go with it."

"This is Prime-choice Colorado beef that you're turning down."

"And I apologize. Maybe I can save it for tomorrow."

Just then he jabbed his fork into the piece of meat and brought it to his plate. "Or I can eat it."

Brooke suddenly burst out laughing, breaking the tension that had been between them since their kisses in the hall. When she finally composed herself, she said, "I guess I don't have to worry about food going to waste with you around."

"Yeah, a dog would starve waiting for my table scraps."

She laughed again. She enjoyed the time she got to spend with this man. She sobered. Too bad it had to end soon. "I should do the dishes." When she tried to stand the muscles in her legs tightened and she let out a groan before she could stop it.

Trent frowned. "Why didn't you tell me you're still sore?"

"That's because I haven't felt any stiffness most of the day. Really, I'm okay."

"I agree, you're more than okay." He winked. "I know something that will help you."

"Another jar of special miracle cure?"

"You might say that. A soak in the Jacuzzi should help the soreness."

"You have a Jacuzzi?"

"I didn't go out and buy one, but my father has had one for years. With all his injuries from his rodeo days, it was the only thing that helped him stay on a horse so he could work the ranch."

She tried not to panic. That was a nice story, but the last thing she needed was to get up close to Trent again. She just wanted to go back to the cabin and dream about his kiss. "I think I'll pass."

He shrugged. "Okay. I was going to ask you to go riding again tomorrow, but I can't risk it."

She froze. "You are a cruel man, Trent Landry. No matter how badly I want to go riding, I'm not going into a Jacuzzi without a suit on."

He stood and picked up their empty plates. "No worries, there are extra suits around here. Laurel has one or two for sure."

She shivered as his heated gaze roamed over her body. "She's about your size."

Brooke worked to slow her breathing. "I guess…" She paused. "You said I could go riding tomorrow."

He nodded and placed their dishes in the sink. "Roundup is coming up. We're riding further out to look for a few stragglers from the herd. I'm pretty sure there's a group of cows hiding out in Rainbow Canyon."

"And you want to take me there?"

"It's an easy ride, and some more of that pretty countryside you like so much. You should be able to handle it just fine."

Trent leaned back against the counter. He folded those muscular arms across his chest. Oh, my, he looked good. She could only imagine him in a pair of trunks with his chest bare…

"So what do you say?"

She shook away her daydream. "Okay, if you think it will help my soreness."

He grinned. "It can't hurt."

Oh, yes, it could. She could sink to the bottom, and she wasn't thinking about the water.

FIFTEEN MINUTES LATER, Trent had changed into his boxer-style trunks and gone outside on the deck off the kitchen and turned on the jets in the Jacuzzi. The temperature had already dropped, but the warm water would keep them warm. The patio was dark, but the area was illuminated from the kitchen lights.

He shook his head and called himself crazy again for suggesting this. The kiss in the hallway had been the first big mistake. Getting involved with Brooke was a bad idea no matter how he rationalized it. He didn't know her, and there was still the chance she could hurt Laurel.

He turned around to discover Brooke standing in the doorway, clutching a towel in front of her. His breath caught as his gaze moved over her modest black one-piece suit. Modest hell. Even in the dim light he could see her breasts were pushing out of the top, and the high-cut spandex showed off far too much skin. All at once he pictured those long shapely legs wrapped around his waist as he made love to her.

"Trent…"

"Hey, I see you found a suit."

"Yes, it's a little small."

He went to her. "Looks fine. Now let's get in before you

freeze." He took her hand and walked her to the steps. "I'll go in first and help you in." He was up and in the water before she could argue, then reached out to her.

She was tentative with the steps so he scooped her up into his arms. "Trent," she gasped.

He enjoyed the feel of her against him. "I didn't want you to fall," he told her.

"Thank you, but you can put me down now."

He pulled her close. "What if I don't want to?"

He felt her tense. "Trent. How can the water help me if you don't let me in it?"

She was right. "Okay, how about this?" He didn't release her, but lowered himself into one of the contoured seats with her on his lap.

She smiled. "Not exactly what I had in mind."

He paused, watching her. Her honey-blond hair was pulled on top of her head held by a clip, showing off her long slender neck and tiny ears. Pretty, yes, but there was a sweet wholesomeness about her that drew him. In the past, he'd always gone for over-the-top sexy types, and definitely a woman who knew the rules: no attachments. Then came Brooke.

"Do you want me to put you in your own seat?"

"I should make you." Her breath was sweet and warm against his face, then she pulled back and their gazes met. She shook her head. "No. Don't stop holding me."

He reached out and cupped her cheek. "Oh, darlin', I want to do much more than just hold you."

Her breath caught and she swallowed hard. "What?"

"Let me show you." He leaned in and brushed his mouth against hers, once twice and then a third time, loving the sound of the tiny catch in her breath. He moved to her neck. "I've wanted to taste your skin all night." He placed tiny kisses along her heated flesh, his tongue taking teasing nibbles along the way. Then he reached her ear and took the lobe into his mouth and sucked gently.

"Trent…"

"Damn, woman, you drive me crazy when you say my name."

He captured her lips with his, and his gentleness turned into hunger. His tongue slipped into her mouth, tasting her and wanting more. His hold tightened, bringing her breasts against his. The rubbing caused a delicious friction. His hand moved up her rib cage and cupped her breast through the suit.

Her head fell against his shoulder and she whimpered his name again.

He pulled the strap down and exposed her to him. "So beautiful." He leaned down and took the hardened nipple in his mouth and she gasped.

He continued the advance on the other breast and she squirmed in his lap, sending a thrill of need through him.

He took her mouth again, and again, brushing, stroking, trying to devour her. His breathing was ragged when he finally broke off the kiss. "I want you, Brooke. I want—"

"Trent, are you out here?" a man's voice bellowed in the dim light.

Trent froze. "Oh, hell." He pulled up Brooke's suit and held her close. "Looks like the Quinns have come home."

Before he could stand the overhead lights came on, showing Rory Quinn in the doorway. Trent moved in front of Brooke. "Hell, Rory, do you mind? Turn off the light."

The older man's gaze went toward Brooke in the hot tub. "What the hell is going on?"

"Turn off the light, Rory."

Suddenly they were concealed in darkness once again.

"Thank you," Trent said. "If you go in my office, I'll be right in."

"I'll be waiting." Finally the man disappeared and Trent sat down beside Brooke. "It's okay, Brooke, he's gone."

"It's not okay. He's going to think I'm just like my mother." She looked at Trent. "You have no idea how many years I've worked to keep people from thinking I'm like her."

Chapter Eleven

Ten minutes later, Brooke was still in the bathroom, and Trent put on his clothes before heading downstairs to the office. He stopped short at the door to find Rory Quinn pacing in front of his father's old desk. Suddenly he noticed how tired the man looked, how much more prominent the lines in his face were. Rory was tall, but his shoulders seemed to be more hunched over these days.

That didn't stifle Trent's anger. "Just what the hell were you doing out there?"

Rory jammed his hands on his hips. "I could ask you the same thing."

Trent came into the room. "I stopped answering for my actions a long time ago, Rory. Besides, I'm not the one barging into a home…uninvited."

Rory lowered his gaze. "Diane and Laurel needed some time, and I was in the way. So I came here hoping to get some answers. Was that Brooke Harper with you?"

"Yes, it was." Trent couldn't help being embarrassed that they'd got caught in a compromising position, but he was more concerned about Brooke.

Rory frowned. "So she's going to seduce you just like her mother did me?"

Rory didn't even know Brooke to compare her to her mother. "You know, maybe this isn't a good time to be discussing this," Trent told him. "How about we talk to-morrow? When you have a chance to cool off."

Without so much as a goodbye, Rory walked out. Maybe that was good. Too many words had been spoken between them. They needed to hold their tongues before they said things that couldn't be taken back. He heard the door close, then the sound of a truck driving off.

Trent combed his fingers through his hair. What the hell just happened? He'd nearly made love to Brooke in a hot tub, that was what happened. He could still feel Brooke's body pressed against his, the taste of her skin on his lips and he hardened with a need he hadn't felt in a long time.

"I'm sorry, Trent."

He swung around to see Brooke standing in his door-way. She was once again dressed in her jeans and blouse. "You have nothing to be sorry for, Brooke." He went to her, but she held him off by raising her hand.

Humiliated, Brooke shifted from one foot to the other. Just what she wanted, for her father to think she was easy. "Rory thinks I'm like my mother. He's never going to let me see Laurel, let alone talk her into coming back to Las Vegas."

Trent gave her a smile that had her aching in need. "You don't know your sister. Laurel does what she wants to do. Besides she's not a child any longer."

"But she's just gone through so much with her groom running off." She didn't want to add any more to the pile. "And what about your business relationship with Rory? I won't come between you two. My mother will have to understand."

Trent crossed the room to her, then reached for her, drawing her close. Brooke started to push him away, but she was weak and needed his strength. He cupped her cheek and leaned down and kissed her, causing her to have the same erotic feeling she'd had in the hot tub.

Before she got totally lost in Trent again, she managed to break his hold and stepped away from temptation. "I have to leave. I don't want to cause you any more trouble."

"So you're just giving up so easily? I expected more of you, Brooke Harper."

"Don't you see it's best for everyone? I stay and I'll just cause more trouble between families that have been friends for years. Rory's relationship with Coralee lasted all of one weekend."

"What about your sister?"

She longed to meet Laurel, but at what cost? "I'll write her a note and explain things."

He shook his head. "You have to do more, Brooke. At least meet Laurel. If she wants you to leave, then go. Don't let Rory's anger keep you from your family."

She looked at Trent and her heart ached. How did he feel? Did he want her to stay, or was he on her father's side?

"You speak with Laurel and if she says no, I'm gone."

Trent looked as though he wanted to argue, but said, "Fair enough. Come on, I'll take you home."

Whether it was a slip of the tongue or not, she wished she could claim Colorado as her home, and one sexy cowboy as her man.

THE FOLLOWING MORNING after chores, Trent walked up to the Quinns' back door as he had all his life. The house had been a second home to him, even after his parents split. This was the first time he felt awkward about the familiarity. Pushing his unease aside he opened the door, calling out as he stepped into the mudroom. He wasn't going to let this come between them.

But it already had. He'd wanted to go straight to Brooke's cabin this morning. They needed to talk also, but this had to be settled first, he owed that much to the Quinns. But after the things Rory had said last night, Trent wasn't sure he could stay neutral.

Diane showed up at the doorway leading to the kitchen. "Hey, you." As usual, she gave him a hug.

The pretty brunette had warm hazel eyes and an inviting smile. He realized he was examining her more closely today. There wasn't any resemblance to her daughter. Now, he knew that was because Laurel looked like her biological mother, Coralee, and her half sister, Brooke.

"Is Rory around?"

"No, he drove into town. He should be back in a few hours."

He wanted to straighten things out with Rory before too much time passed.

"I'll come back." He started to leave when Diane called him back.

"Thank you, Trent, for taking care of things here," Diane told him. "I know we left in a hurry."

"Not a problem." He wasn't sure if she was talking about the abandoned wedding or not, but he was staying on the safer topic. "Chet and some of the hands packed up the tables and chairs. We donated the food and flowers to a church shelter, except what we held back for the guys here. At least they got a great meal that night." He glanced around. "How is Laurel doing?"

"You know her. She acts like things don't bother her, and then she goes and takes off to be alone. Right now, she's riding that crazy stallion of hers."

"Capture the Wind?" Trent envied her the beautiful bay stallion. His good bloodlines were great for acquiring high stud fees.

Diane nodded. "I wish Rory would just sell the rogue. Do you know how many times she's been bucked off the animal?"

Trent tried not to smile and lost. "She does love her horses. It's part of her job."

"Until she breaks her neck." Diane went to the coffeepot and poured two cups. She handed one to him. "Rory said you were with that woman last night."

Now his personal life was an open book. "That woman's name is Brooke Harper. She's Laurel's sister."

"She claims to be," Diane corrected.

"Wait until you see her. The resemblance to Laurel is remarkable."

The older woman looked sad. "Why did all this have to happen, Trent? First Jack, and now, this woman coming here. Laurel won't even talk to me right now."

"If you mean Brooke Harper, isn't it Laurel's decision to tell her to leave?"

Diane shook her head. "We can't let Coralee Harper into our lives again. I suffered through the woman's manipulation before. I won't let her do it again."

Trent couldn't help wondering if Coralee had made trouble even after the custody agreement. "You do know Coralee is in a care facility with Alzheimer's? She can't hurt you."

A tear found its way down Diane's cheek. "She already has. I've lost my daughter."

It was midmorning and Brooke hadn't heard a word from Trent since he'd taken her back to the cabin last night. Sadness washed over her as she recalled the tenderness of his kisses, his touch. She shivered, but wouldn't allow herself to linger over what would never be.

After Rory found them together in the hot tub, she

knew any chance of her being welcomed here was gone. She tossed the rest of her clothes into her suitcase. No use waiting around to get kicked off the property. She had more pride than that.

Crazy thing. It didn't matter if she didn't want to leave. She had to. Trent wasn't a man she needed to get involved with. Too bad for her that it was already too late to pull back on those feelings. She just had to make sure that no matter what, she didn't jeopardize his relationship with the Quinns. If and when Laurel and Rory learned the entire truth, Trent shouldn't be caught in the middle of everything.

She carried her bag out of the bedroom and glanced back at the bed. The sheets had been stripped off, and the blanket was neatly folded at the end. Walking down the hall, she eyed the spotless kitchen. She refused to leave a mess.

There was a knock on the door and she paused. She wanted it to be Trent, but then again, she didn't, because saying goodbye to him was going to hurt.

Brooke released a slow breath, hoping she could find the words that would help her leave without making a fool of herself. She pulled open the door and was shocked to find a familiar-looking woman standing on the porch. They did look a lot alike.

Laurel Quinn was a tall, striking woman with long wheat-blond hair pulled back into a long braid. And big green eyes with long lashes.

She had an amused look on her face. "Well, damn. I guess it's true when they say we all have a twin."

Brooke's heart pounded loudly in her ears. Did she know? "Excuse me?"

"I meant we do look alike," Laurel clarified. "Hi, I'm Laurel. I hear you're my long-lost sister."

Emotions surfaced and tears formed in Brooke's eyes. Her sister. She blinked them away. She never cried, not even when meeting her twin sister for the first time.

This was awkward. "I'm Brooke Harper." Brooke held out her hand and Laurel seemed grateful to shake it.

She looked toward the porch railing and saw the magnificent stallion tied there. The horse's body was a slick golden brown with a black mane and tail. Impatient, the animal stomped the ground. "Who's your friend?"

"Capture the Wind. I call him Wind."

The animal whinnied on hearing his name. "Typical man, wants attention all the time."

Brooke had a feeling Laurel wasn't just talking about horses. She walked to the animal. "May I pet him?"

"Sure."

Laurel Quinn held the bridle so Brooke could run her hand over the equine's forehead. She was glad they had the demanding stallion to concentrate on, because she had no idea what to say to her newfound sister. She couldn't help staring at Brooke Harper. They did look amazingly alike for half sisters. Their eyes, the shape of their faces, even their height and build. She loved that fact.

Even only knowing for the past twenty-four hours hadn't helped ease the excitement, or the pain of so many lost years. Yet, now she didn't want to waste time harping on the secrets her parent had kept. For now, she only wanted to explore their chance to get to know each other.

The big horse ate up the attention. Laurel held on to the bridle so as not to frighten Brooke. The animal still managed to nudge her, causing her to stumble backward some, but she came back for more. Her sister just came up several notches in Laurel's book.

"He's beautiful," Brooke said.

"And he knows it." Laurel stroked the animal lovingly.

"He's also cocky as hell." Giving Wind attention helped break the awkwardness between them. Finally she said, "Sorry I wasn't here when you arrived, but you probably heard, I've been chasing after my runaway groom."

Brooke's gaze met hers, but there wasn't any pitying look. "I'm sorry that didn't work out."

Laurel shrugged. "It's for the best."

Brooke sighed. "Then I show up and dump all this stuff on you. Please, come inside. Maybe we can talk a little?"

"Yeah, it seems we might have some catching up to do."

Laurel knew that Wind wasn't going to contentedly stay tied to the porch. She looked off in the distance to see Larry on one of the horses, then stuck her fingers in her mouth and whistled. Then when he turned to her she motioned for him to come to her.

"I'll have Larry take Wind back to the barn."

When the ranch hand appeared on horseback, Laurel handed him Wind's reins and gave him instructions for the horse.

"Not a problem, Laurel." The young man turned to Brooke. "Good to see you again, Brooke."

"Nice to see you again, too, Larry," Brooke said.

He rode off with the stallion in tow. And Brooke quickly explained. "I arrived when they were removing the tables and chairs from the wedding. I sort of helped."

It was bad enough she had to live with a groom who didn't show up, but the new sister had helped in the cleanup, too. "Wow, you drive all this way to meet me and the first thing you get put to work."

Brooke shook her head. "I didn't mind, really. And besides, your family gave me a place to stay."

Laurel refused to comment on that statement. Instead she walked into the cabin and saw the suitcase. "The accommodations must be bad if you're leaving."

Brooke seemed to have trouble making eye contact. "Your father is pretty upset about me coming here. I thought it might be best if I went back to Las Vegas."

Trying to hold on to her anger, she said, "I thought you wanted to meet me."

"I did," Brooke insisted. "I mean I do, but I seem to be causing problems, especially for your father."

Her father's recent actions were so unlike him. "Dad's a little gruff sometimes. But he's got a heart of gold." Laurel sighed. "You see, I was a sick kid. Bad asthma." She remembered how at the age of seven she'd begged her parents to allow her to learn to ride a horse like her friends. "I spent a lot of time in the hospital and both my parents have become a little overprotective."

"That's understandable," Brooke agreed. "Would you like something to drink? I think there's water."

"Water sounds great."

Brooke went to the small refrigerator and took out two bottles. They sat down on the sofa.

Laurel twisted off the lid. "So, you've been here since Saturday?"

"Yes, when I arrived at the house there were all these flowers and ribbons everywhere. I should have left, but instead went out back to find a beautiful setup for a wedding."

Over the past few days, she realized she'd been more angry than sad. "It might have been if I'd picked a different guy to marry."

"Sorry," Brooke apologized. "I know this has to be painful for you."

"Not as much as I thought. I'm just so angry." Laurel waved a hand. "Tell me, how long have you known about me?"

"Not long, only a few weeks. I'm not sure how much

you know about our...biological mother, but she has been diagnosed with early-onset Alzheimer's. Six months ago, I had to put her in a care facility. That's when she started talking about her baby Laurel. Of course, I thought she was just confused, because a lot she said lately hadn't been making sense. But she mentioned your father, Rory Quinn."

Brooke wanted to tell Laurel everything, but after their father's reaction last night, she couldn't. "Then I found your birth certificate and the legal papers, granting your father full custody of Laurel Kathryn Harper."

"My father said he met Coralee at the National Rodeo Finals in Las Vegas. He also explained that he'd had a fight with my mother—I mean Diane—and they'd broken up."

Laurel shook her head, looking a bit dazed. "It wasn't easy to take this all in. Three days ago, I knew my family, my mother and father. Now I discover I've been lied to all these years."

And Brooke didn't want to add to the confusion. She was also afraid that she would say too much. "I don't know much about what happened, either. And now Coralee's memory is fading quickly. She wants to explain to you why she gave you away."

"Seems both our parents neglected to tell us some important details about our lives."

"Don't blame your parents."

"Who do I blame?"

"Coralee—she gave you away, but from what I can see, you were the lucky one."

EARLY AFTERNOON, TRENT was going over building plans at the construction site, but his thoughts weren't on business. He hadn't been able to get Brooke out of his head since he'd dropped her off at the cabin last night. It had taken every ounce of self-control not to follow her inside and finish what they'd started in the hot tub.

Waking up this morning on that damn airbed and aching for the woman wasn't much better. Instead he'd gone to the Bucking Q's horse barn to find Laurel. He found her busy, exercising her beloved quarter horses. Laurel's way to handle problems. When she tried to say she was too busy to talk to him, he wouldn't allow it. They needed to talk about what happened the past week.

Had it been only four days since Laurel cancelled her wedding? Then the beautiful Brooke Harper had shown up on the Quinns' doorstep.

Laurel was probably torn about what to do. He'd urged her to go talk to Brooke to learn more.

About an hour ago, he was happy to see her riding by on her bay stallion and headed for the cabin.

"Now, if I can keep my mind on work, something might get done," he murmured as he looked over the building plans spread out on the table.

"I see you got things moving again," a familiar voice said.

Trent looked up to see Rory standing in the doorway. *Okay, here we go.* "I received another loan from the bank, and decided if we didn't want to lose our total investment, we need to finish the rest of the buildings."

The older man nodded. "Just so you know, I'm going to pay you back for everything."

"You will not. We both got taken by Aldrich. Besides, you invested more money than I did to begin with. We get the structure finished and rented out, we can pay the loan off."

"What's the new timeline on completion?"

"The outside, about three weeks. Inside, that depends

on the crew." He pointed to the two completed cabins where he and Brooke had been staying. "We can rent those two cabins immediately."

"So Coralee's daughter is leaving?"

Trent released a breath. Why was it so hard to say her name? "Brooke Harper."

"Yes. Is she leaving soon?"

"When you were in Denver, you wanted her to stay. Now you can't wait to have her gone. Why don't you just talk to her and maybe it'll resolve any misconceptions about why she came here?"

Rory diverted his gaze. "You don't understand. There are so many bad memories associated with her mother. She almost destroyed my marriage twice."

"Brooke wasn't even born then."

"But she's Coralee's daughter."

"So is Laurel."

Rory took off his hat and ran a hand over his short gray hair. "Okay, but she's here because of Coralee."

"The woman has Alzheimer's. That much is true, because my PI, Cody Marsh, verified it."

"What did he find out about Brooke?"

"I told you, nothing yet. Give it a few more days. And be happy to have your family here. Also the fact that Laurel didn't marry Aldrich."

That got Rory to smile. "Damn, we did dodge a bullet on that one."

"So let Laurel talk with Brooke. After all, they are sisters. It's important that they have some time together."

Rory studied him for a moment. "You still think about your brother, don't you?"

Trent still thought of Chris; the passing of the years hadn't changed that. "Yeah, and coming back to the ranch makes it harder sometimes."

Rory sighed. "Twenty years is a long time to keep blaming yourself, son."

Trent's chest tightened. "I only blame myself because Chris's death was my fault, and I have to live with that fact."

Chapter Twelve

Later that afternoon, after Laurel had left the cabin, Brooke called the care facility to talk with her mother. Erin cautioned her that Coralee had been having a bad few days.

Brooke braced herself when her mother's voice came over the line.

"Why haven't you called me?" Coralee demanded, skipping through any kind of greeting.

"I have called, Mother. Yesterday. You were taking a nap."

"No one told me," she said, irritated. "Well, did you see Laurel? Is she pretty? Is she asking about me?"

Brooke shut her eyes, and rested her head on the sofa. "Yes, Mother, I finally met Laurel today. And she's very pretty and she looks like you."

Her mother sighed. "Oh, I knew she would be pretty. So are you bringing her home today?"

"Not today, Mother. Not yet."

"But you promised. You said you'd bring her. I need to see her." Coralee's agitation rose.

"I said I'll try," Brooke soothed in a low, calming voice.

"No! She has to come and see me. Why are you being hateful, Brooke? You're just a hateful child! I want my daughter. I want Laurel now."

Heart pounding, Brooke felt the tears burning behind

her eyelids. She started to speak when she heard Erin's voice.

"Brooke. I need to give Coralee her medication, then put her to bed. We'll talk later."

"Thank you, Erin. Goodbye."

Brooke closed her phone and allowed the tears to flow freely. She knew Coralee was ill, that this disease was destroying her. Then why did her words hurt so much?

All her life, Coralee had made Brooke feel she was never good enough…she was never smart enough…never pretty enough. She couldn't blame that on the disease.

Her thoughts turned to Laurel. Her twin. She'd enjoyed their talk earlier. She was nice, and didn't seem to resent her coming here.

So why hadn't Brooke just shown her their birth certificates? Then she'd know that they were full sisters. Was she hoping that Laurel would feel a special connection between them? Maybe that was too much to ask after only one meeting.

Brooke stood. She was more worried that Laurel wouldn't go back to Las Vegas if she knew the whole truth about their mother. By just coming here, Brooke had already taken away Laurel's mother, and replaced her with a second-rate lounge singer who had been an alcoholic. Not fair.

And yes, Brooke was envious of the good life her sister had here with Rory. From what she'd seen and heard, her father adored Laurel. What would it be like to feel that kind of unconditional love?

How could she ask her to share their father? Would Brooke even fit in here if the Quinns did ask her to stay? Now she was dreaming.

Darn it, Coralee. Why did you have to do this? I'd lived without a father this long… A tear found its way down her cheek, then another. She absently wiped them away, hating that she let this get to her. That had been how she'd survived, by not letting things get to her.

It would be best if she just walked away from everyone: her sister, father…and Trent. To stop dreaming about a life here, a life where she didn't have to struggle to make a living, to stay in school, to keep searching for the elusive love in her mother's eyes.

She stood and struggled to suck air into her lungs. "No, don't let it get to you." She recited the familiar chant that kept her going. "Don't let 'em see how much it hurts you."

She walked slowly through the cabin, doing some relaxing breathing exercises. She'd get through this, then go back to her life.

There was a knock on the door, but she ignored it. She couldn't see anyone now.

The knock came again. "Brooke?"

Trent.

"I know you're in there," he called through the closed door.

Oh, God. She couldn't see him like this. She went to the door. "Trent, I don't feel well."

"Brooke, we need to talk. I won't take long. Please, open the door."

She was weak when it came to this man. She did as he asked and let him in.

Trent crossed the threshold and wrapped her in a tight embrace. He was so relieved she was still here. Laurel had let it slip about seeing the packed suitcase.

He pulled back and saw her puffy eyes. She'd been crying. "Are you okay?" He touched her cheek. "Did someone say something to you?"

"If you're talking about Rory, no, I haven't seen him

since last night…" She glanced away. "I just got off the phone with my mother. She's having a rough day."

Trent hated seeing Brooke like this. He reached for her and wrapped his arms around her again. "Oh, babe, I wish I could make it better." He rubbed her back and could feel her starting to relax.

After a few minutes, Brooke pulled back, once again composed. "Why are you here?"

Was she upset because he hadn't come by earlier? "When I saw Laurel this morning, she said she was going to come by. I wanted to give you both some time. How was it between you two?"

"She's nice. She doesn't seem angry that I'm here."

He couldn't hide his smile. "I knew you'd like her." His gaze moved over her face and the uncanny resemblance to Laurel. Their hair was a different shade of blond, but their eyes were about the same color and shape, and their jawlines were similar.

Brooke stood and walked across the room to the window. "This has been a nice trip, Trent, but I realized after talking to Coralee today, I need to get back home."

Trent went to her. The last thing he wanted was for Brooke to leave, not yet. He wanted to at least figure out what this was between them. Then what? What would he do? He wasn't sure. Brooke made him feel things for the first time in a long time.

"I thought you said you were going to stay through the weekend? And there's the roundup in two days."

She shrugged, but he caught the spark of excitement in those green eyes. "That was before I knew when the Quinns were returning. They're home now. I've met Laurel, and now she knows the situation with our mother. She has to make the choice to come see her or not."

"What about Rory, and Diane?"

She shook her head. "They don't want to meet me. They hate my mother, and they think I'm just like her." She tried to hide it, but he saw the hurt and pain in her eyes.

"Then prove them wrong, Brooke," he told her.

She looked at him. "Seems that's what I've been doing all my life. When do I stop paying for my mother's sins?"

THAT EVENING, TRENT drove Brooke up to the Quinns' home. Laurel had called two hours earlier with an invitation to supper.

Brooke didn't want to accept, but Trent had strongly encouraged her to go, saying he would be right beside her. He wasn't going to let anything happen to her. She wasn't so sure. As far as the Quinns knew, she wasn't any blood to them. And she hadn't decided if they were ever going to find out. She couldn't take that chance.

Trent helped her out of the truck. She smoothed the imaginary wrinkles from her long black skirt and straightened her large cable-knit sweater. She was also wearing her black low-heel boots.

One of the few nice outfits she'd brought on the trip. Not that she had a closet full of clothes at home.

She felt Trent's hand engulf hers. "It's going to be okay, Brooke. Relax."

She nodded, but her gut told her that this could be a lot worse than even dealing with Coralee's rage. "I'll try."

They walked up the back steps through the mudroom and into the kitchen. Brooke was familiar with this room, since she and Trent had had a meal here the day she arrived.

Trent called out a greeting and Laurel appeared in the doorway. "Oh, good, you made it." She hugged Trent first, then Brooke. "I'm glad you're here. My parents are nice people. It's just this is a shock for them, and not long after the other shock of my cancelled wedding."

Brooke nodded. "I don't mean to add more. That's the reason I shouldn't have come."

Laurel tugged on her arm. "Oh, no, you don't. You're my sister now, and if there's any chance of us having a relationship, we all need to get along."

Trent added. "She's right, Brooke. She's a package deal."

Laurel began to laugh, and Brooke couldn't help smiling, too.

Laurel punched Trent in the arm playfully. "Good analogy, soldier boy."

"Hey, don't disrespect me. That's sergeant major to you, missy."

Laurel wrinkled her nose. "Don't call me that."

Although Brooke loved their banter, she also envied how these two got along. Obviously they were longtime friends.

"Say, when are we going to eat?"

"Come on in," Laurel encouraged. "Just follow the spicy scent of Mom's Mexican casserole."

Brooke felt her anxiety return when they walked through the kitchen and into the dining room where a large table was set for five.

She heard voices then a small dark-haired woman turned around. Behind her was a tall slender man. Her breath caught as her gaze moved over him. His auburn hair was streaked with gray, but still thick and wavy. His rosy complexion had tiny lines around those green eyes that mirrored hers. Oh, God. He was her father.

Trent was the first to speak. "Diane and Rory, I'd like you to meet Brooke Harper. Brooke, Diane and Rory."

Brooke spoke first. "Thank you for having me to your home and allowing me to stay in your cabin."

The couple nodded, then Rory's gaze went to her, then to his daughter. His eyes grew large. "You do look like Laurel. What about your father—"

"Rory," Trent began. "That doesn't matter. She's here for Laurel."

Brooke took a step closer and raised her chin. "To answer your question, Mr. Quinn, I honestly don't know my father." That was the truth. She didn't know this man.

He glanced away and his wife took over. "Why don't we sit down? Laurel, come help me bring over the food from the sideboard."

Brooke said, "I could help, too."

Not overly friendly, Diane shook her head. "No, you're a guest. This will only take a minute." Laurel shrugged and followed her mother.

Heart pounding, Brooke turned around, but stayed close to Trent. He was her lifeline.

"How long will you be staying in Colorado?"

Don't act hurt. "Now that I was able to contact Laurel, I can leave tomorrow—"

"Brooke's not going anywhere yet," Trent said. "I talked her into staying through the roundup."

Laurel came to the table, carrying a big dish. "And I'm going to teach her how to ride."

"Hey, I taught her already," Trent added as he relieved Diane of her burden, a big bowl of beans and some warm tortillas. He placed them on the table and escorted Brooke to her seat.

"Here, you sit next to me." He pulled out her chair for her, then sat down beside her. He reached for her hand under the table and whispered, "You're doing fine."

She let out a soft breath. "Thank you." She looked at

Rory at the head of the table. Diane was on his right and Laurel was beside her mother and across from Brooke.

After a simple blessing, they had a quiet dinner, but Brooke couldn't seem to stir up an appetite as she listened to the men talk about the roundup. They'd planned to combine both ranches' branding and inoculating the calves. Also, they discussed the timeline for the cabins so they could begin to advertise.

Trent turned the attention to Brooke. "You didn't know, but Brooke has just received her degree in hotel management. She has some suggestions for the hunting lodge. Ideas on who to advertise to and what to add to our website."

Brooke could see Rory's anger, but he managed to control it and said, "I don't think Brooke needs to concern herself with our website. After all, she'll be returning to Las Vegas in a few days."

A sudden ache squeezed her heart. Rory Quinn wanted her gone. Even though he didn't know who she really was, it still hurt.

Before Trent could defend her yet again, she touched his arm. "No, Trent. Mr. Quinn is right, he doesn't need my input. This is his project, too." She stood. "Thank you both for dinner." She worked hard to smile at Laurel. "It was great meeting you, Laurel, but I think it's best I leave." She glanced at Trent. "Trent, you stay, please. I'm not feeling like company."

She stood and walked out of the room. If anything, her mother had taught her how to make an exit. Once outside in the fresh air, she felt her resolve shatter. She hated that Coralee had sent her to this place, and for what? To take the blame for something that happened all those years ago. She had no part in it.

She started down the driveway, but stopped on hearing her name called. She turned and saw Laurel coming after her.

"Hey, I don't blame you for leaving," her sister said. "I've never seen my parents act like that, and Trent is letting Dad know that he didn't like what happened. But please, Brooke, don't leave the ranch. I know you have to get back, but I'm only asking for a few days. I want to get to know you. We're sisters. And I'm hoping not just because you want me to meet Coralee, but because you want us to have a relationship, too."

Brooke was touched. "I would like that very much."

Laurel beamed. "How about we start with a slumber party? Your cabin, say in an hour?"

Brooke's heart was about ready to burst. "Can you get your hands on some popcorn? I'm suddenly hungry."

AROUND TEN O'CLOCK, Trent was at his house, nursing his second beer since he'd left Brooke in Laurel's care at the cabin. And he'd been left out cold and alone.

Any way you looked at it, tonight's dinner had been a disaster. No way could he talk Rory and Diane into accepting Brooke. Question was how far would the couple go in persuading Laurel not to see Coralee? So where did that leave Brooke? Back in Las Vegas, and he'd be here. Alone. In this house.

He took a long pull on his beer. Why did it matter? He'd been alone since he was thirteen when Chris died. Twenty years. He closed his eyes and his chest squeezed so tight he had trouble drawing his next breath. He still missed his little brother. He missed the happy family that used to live in this house, too.

For years, he'd fought wars and terrorists all over the world, seen comrades die, even in his arms. But when he'd come home, he was brought to his knees seeing his young brother's grave. Nothing he'd done helped erase the guilt he'd felt for leaving Chris behind all those years ago.

Suddenly his phone rang and he pulled it out of his pocket and saw Brooke's name. "Brooke?"

"No, silly, it's Laurel." She giggled. "You hunk a hunk of burning love."

Someone had been drinking. "Laurel? What are you two doing?"

"I'm getting to know my little sister. Thank you for keeping her here so I could meet her." She giggled again. "Can you believe it, I have a sister."

"Yeah, I can believe it." He smiled. "Where's Brooke?"

"She's in the bathroom. But we've been comparing notes about the men in our lives. My guy, that SOB, I really ragged on, but you, soldier boy, are one of the good guys. And guess what, I think Brooke really likes you, too. Oh, God, did that just sound like high school?"

Before Trent could answer, he heard another voice, then Brooke came on the phone. "Trent, I can't believe Laurel called you."

"Better me than someone else. Are you two okay?"

There was a long pause, then Brooke said, "We've had a few glasses of wine, but we're fine."

"Good." He hesitated, not wanting to hang up. "I miss you."

"I shouldn't tell you, but I miss you, too," she admitted.

The phone to his ear, he walked through the kitchen and turned on the light to the deck. "I keep thinking about last night. I'm looking out at the hot tub and can imagine us there, together. I can still hear your soft moans as I touched you, as I tasted your smooth skin." His body stirred, but he kept on going. "Do you know how badly I want to make love to you?"

He heard her sharp intake of breath. "That can't happen, Trent. I'm leaving soon."

"I know. It's probably not wise for us to think past the roundup," he agreed. "Of course, you could come back to visit, or I can come to Las Vegas."

"I'll have a new job, and not much time."

He heard Laurel's voice in the background and he wasn't in the mood to hear any more excuses. "I should let you go. Good night, Brooke."

He hung up and decided he needed to go to bed. If he could get through the next few days with Brooke, then send her home, maybe things might get back to normal. Yeah, right. He didn't see that happening.

Chapter Thirteen

A day and a half later the roundup began at dawn. Trent, Mike and Ricky had arrived at the Bucking Q with their horses, and ready for the cattle drive to begin.

The morning started out cool and a little dry. The bawling cows and calves kicked up enough dust to have the hands riding drag wearing neckerchiefs. That would be Brooke and Laurel and Ricky. The kid had to be where the girls were. Trent and Mike rode flank and Bucking Q's Chet and Larry took the point position. Of course, Rory was trail boss, and a few of their neighbors, Henry Clark and Jack Hendricks, filled in where they were needed. There would be more people when they got to the branding pens.

Trent turned toward the back of the herd on hearing Laurel's excited voice.

"That's it," she called to Brooke from atop her cutting horse, Starr Gazer. "Go get 'em," she encouraged her newfound sister as Brooke took off on Raven after a calf. He watched amazed at Brooke's ability. She'd taken to riding as if she were born to it. And she enjoyed it, too.

Trent smiled with pride when she managed to corral the small animal and send him scurrying back to his mama.

Ricky and Chet cheered her on as she fell back into

her position. He caught a blush over the top of the scarf that covered part of her face.

"She's not half bad on a horse."

Trent turned to find Rory beside him. "Yeah, and she's only had a few days of experience."

Rory nodded as he rode alongside Trent. "Laurel was working with her all day yesterday. I saw them in the corral." They rode along with the slow-moving herd. "Have you heard any more news from your friend the PI?"

Trent had received a text, but he couldn't call Cody until tonight. "Not yet." He studied Rory. "What are you expecting to find? For Brooke to have a police record, or maybe she was wanted by the law?"

Rory glared. "I just want to know if she's trying to play me like her mother did."

Trent frowned. "Has Brooke asked you for anything?"

Rory kept quiet, staring ahead.

"I told you Coralee is in a care facility. She can't hurt you or Laurel. From what I know about Brooke, she is who she says she is. A recent college graduate, and trying to make her mother's—who's dealing with Alzheimer's— life a little better by granting her this wish." Who was he trying to convince, Rory or himself?

"This isn't the first time Coralee has disrupted our lives," Rory began. "Twenty-eight years ago, out of the blue, I get a call from her, telling me I fathered a daughter. Then in the next breath, she offered me custody. The next day, Diane and I were on a plane to get Laurel before Coralee changed her mind.

"When Coralee showed up with four-month-old Laurel, she was frail and weak with an ignored asthma condition, but Coralee wouldn't hand her over to me yet. It took several thousand dollars just to get my daughter. She said it was to pay for medical bills."

"Why didn't you go to court?"

Rory looked sad. "Truth was Laurel was so sickly, I was afraid something would happen to her before we could get her medical attention. So we paid." His gaze went to his daughter riding next to Brooke. "I don't regret a minute, or a dollar of the money it took to get her. We've had Laurel all these years."

"Is that why you never told Laurel about her birth mother?"

Rory looked all of his sixty-one years. "There were other reasons, too. I hated the fact that I'd been unfaithful to Diane. I mean, we weren't married at the time, and we had this big fight before I took off for the National Finals. After your dad and I won for team calf roping, Wade went back to the hotel, and I went to a bar to celebrate alone. Coralee Harper was at the piano singing…"

Rory paused and the only sounds were from the cattle bawling and men shouting out commands. "She gave me attention and I ate it up. Afterward, I felt sick. I went home to Diane, confessed everything. She forgave me and I asked her to marry me.

"We bought the Bucking Q and I thought life would be perfect for us." He smiled. "Diane got pregnant right away, but then she lost the baby. Worse, there were complications that made it impossible for her to have any more children."

"I'm sorry, Rory."

Trent shifted in the saddle and guided his horse away from the herd, but his gaze stayed sharp on his job.

Rory continued. "So when Laurel was given to us, Diane didn't bat an eye whether or not to keep her as her own child. They bonded from the beginning. When Coralee came around when Laurel was five years old, we paid her off again, but this time we had a lawyer draw up the papers to keep Coralee away permanently. That was the last money she got from us."

Trent nodded, understanding his friend's pain.

"Now, Laurel is grown, and Coralee is asking to see her. Why? You said it's because she regrets giving her daughter away, but I can't trust her, and until I know otherwise, that includes Brooke, too."

AFTER TWO HOURS in the saddle Brooke was exhausted, but didn't want to quit. She loved riding. There was something therapeutic about the gentle rocking with the horse's easy rhythm. And getting to spend time with Laurel was a bonus.

She felt almost giddy.

And then there was Trent. She glanced across the herd to see him on Rango, working at the flank position. He looked at her and waved. She waved back, eyeing the cowboy's expertise on horseback. The man did more than warm a girl's heart; there were a few other places that got all warm and tingly.

Hearing her name called, Brooke came out of her daydream and saw a calf had taken off.

"Oh, no, you don't." She dug her heels into Raven and the mare shot off after the tiny bovine. She nearly caught up to the bawling calf, but suddenly the animal fell when it got caught in some downed fencing in the underbrush. *Oh, no.* Not wanting her horse tangled in the wire, Brooke pulled sharply on the reins. Raven stopped immediately, but Brooke went flying in the air and hit the ground hard.

She groaned, feeling pain shoot along her spine and shoulders. Even her chest hurt. Unable to cry with the pain, she concentrated on trying to breathe, but nothing worked. Was she going to die?

Heart hammering, Trent raced up on Rango, jumped

off and was at Brooke's side in seconds. He tugged the bandanna down. "Brooke. Talk to me, babe."

"Can't," she gasped for air. She opened her eyes, showing her panic.

"Breathe slowly. You got the wind knocked out of you."

Removing his gloves, Trent moved his hands over Brooke's limbs, checking for any broken bones. There weren't any, thank God. Then he began to examine her skull, looking for any sign of blood. When he found none, he felt for bumps. None, again. Relief washed over him.

"How is she?" Ricky asked as he jumped off his horse along with Laurel just behind him.

"Hey, Brooke. You okay?" Laurel asked as she knelt down on the other side of her.

Brooke nodded. "Just terrific."

Trent watched as Brooke's breathing slowly improved. He exhaled a sigh of relief. "Better now?"

Brooke glanced around to see everyone crowding around her. "I just feel stupid. How's the calf? Raven?"

She tried to get up, but Trent placed a hand on her to stop her. "The calf will survive, and Raven wasn't hurt. You, on the other hand, might be."

"Not my finest moment, but I didn't hurt anything important."

Damn, stubborn woman wouldn't take help. "Okay, just sit up first, but if you're dizzy you're not getting back on the horse."

Trent wrapped an arm around her shoulders and helped her into a sitting position.

Ricky handed her her cowboy hat. "Ah, she's okay." He winked at her and climbed back on his mount.

Brooke felt the heat on her face and it had nothing to do with the sun. She took Trent's offered hand, and let him pull her up, then he placed her hat on her head.

"Good job chasing down the calf, but your dismount needs some work," Laurel said with a chuckle.

Brooke couldn't help laughing. "One thing's for sure, Raven has good brakes." She walked over to her horse. "Don't ya, girl? You did good." She rubbed the horse's neck and got a loud whinny.

Brooke grabbed the reins, jammed her booted foot into the stirrup and swung back into the saddle. She wheeled Raven around in time to discover Rory headed her way.

Astride his big gray gelding, he came up beside her. His gaze moved over her. She felt a surge of happiness seeing his concern. "How do you feel?"

"Really, I'm fine." She hesitated. "Are you going to take me off the roundup?"

If so, she'd have to go back to the cabin alone. Since she was leaving in a few days, this would be her only opportunity to be with…family.

Rory shifted in the saddle. "No, you weren't being reckless. Good job handling your horse. Besides, most riders take falls." He turned in the saddle and called over his shoulder. "Chet, you get some of the men out here tomorrow to clear away that old fence. I don't want anyone else hurt."

Rory turned back to her. "Just be careful from now on." He tugged on the reins and his horse took off back to the herd. She fought hard to keep from calling after him, telling him who she was, but the words died in her throat. She doubted she'd ever get the chance to call him father.

SHORTLY AFTER BROOKE'S FALL, the crew finally got the herd to the branding pens by early afternoon. Side by side, Brooke and Laurel finished off the drive by directing the last of the calves into a separate pen to be vaccinated, tagged, and the males castrated. The bawling intensified after the division of mamas and babies. It was heart-wrenching.

The men took a break for a quick lunch of sandwiches and drinks, then went right back to work. Brooke wanted nothing to do with this part of the roundup. She and Laurel tended to the horses and stayed out of the sun, letting the men handle the branding.

Of course, she enjoyed watching Trent. That seemed to be her favorite pastime these days. Astride his horse, lariat in hand and with only the flick of his wrist, he could rope the hind legs of a small calf. A thrill shot through her. It was a sight to see.

"He's not hard on the eyes at all." Laurel nodded toward the branding area, then continued to brush her horse, Starr.

Brooke looked up to see Laurel watching her. She just continued grooming Raven. She wasn't going to get on the topic of Trent.

"It's all fascinating," she said. "I've never seen cattle getting branded. Does it hurt them?"

Laurel nodded. "It does, but not for long. I'm sure that you could ask Dad, or Trent would probably be happy to explain everything to you."

"I don't want to bother him."

Laurel chuckled. "You've managed to do that already. The man can't take his eyes off you. I'm a little jealous."

Brooke froze. Laurel had feelings for Trent? "You and Trent? I mean, you were going to marry…"

Laurel walked around Starr toward Brooke. She absently stroked Raven's rump as she grinned. "Stop looking so worried. I haven't had a thing for Trent Landry since I was fourteen, and he came to visit his dad while in the army. Damn, he did look good in uniform."

Brooke could imagine.

"As for Jack Aldrich, not my finest moment. Now I realize, I liked the idea of falling in love more than actually being in love. And when Jack came along, he knew the right things to say to me. He fed into my lifelong dream of raising and training quarter horses." She shrugged. "In the end, I'm totally grateful that he couldn't go through with marrying me. Too bad he had no problem taking Trent's and Dad's money."

"You can't blame yourself, Laurel. Men like Jack know exactly how to draw people in." She knew that because Coralee found a lot of Jack Aldriches.

"Coralee didn't have much luck with men, either."

"What about Rory?"

Brooke wasn't sure how much to tell her. "Honestly, I had never heard about Rory Quinn until about a month ago. Then at Trent's house, I saw the picture of your father with Wade Landry. He was a good-looking man, and being a rodeo star was what probably attracted our mother to him." Brooke saw the hopeful look in Laurel's eyes. "The thing with Coralee, Laurel, she only wanted to have a career, to make it big as a singer. That's probably the reason why she gave your father custody."

"Did she?" Laurel asked. "I mean, did she ever have success at singing?"

Their time at the cabin the other night hadn't covered much of this. Laurel had been more interested in Brooke.

Brooke glanced away, thinking about all the things her childhood lacked because of their mother's obsession.

"Not really. She was a backup singer in her younger years, but as she got older, her voice became weaker, so she mostly worked as a waitress."

Laurel paused a moment, then said, "Dad told me she wasn't a nice person."

Brooke knew Rory felt the same way about her, too. "Coralee needed to be the center of attention." She shrugged. "I guess I'm just used to her that way."

"That couldn't have been easy on you."

She didn't want to talk about Coralee anymore. "Like I said, it's what you get used to." She glanced toward the pens. "Do you want to wander over and see if the guys are finished with the branding?"

Laurel nodded. "Sure. I'll go."

Together, they walked to the fence in time to see a calf being wrestled to the ground. One man shot the animal with a needle, another man tagged the ear, then the last one took the red-hot branding iron and pressed it to the calf's hip. The smell of burning fur assaulted her nose. Finally the animal was released to go into the pen with its mama.

Her attention went to Trent on his horse as he swung his rope overhead, then he let the lasso fly and caught another calf's hind legs. Tying his end of the rope to the saddle horn, he dragged the animal into the branding area.

"Now there's a man worth taking a risk on. Trent's a little rough around the edges from all the years in the military, but he's a good guy. It's sad about his dad. I think they left a lot of things unsaid, and never had the chance to fix their relationship. A lot of that had to do with Chris dying. It tore the family apart." Laurel looked at her. "I bet a good woman in his life could make all the difference."

"What are you trying to say?" Brooke asked.

"Just saying that you should explore your opportunities during the short time you're here."

Brooke knew she was developing feelings for Trent already. Dear Lord, she hadn't even known the man a week. "I like him, but I'm not the-spur-of-the-moment-fling type."

Laurel arched an eyebrow. "Maybe you should consider

changing that. I haven't seen Trent date any woman in a long time. And I've seen the looks he gives you, like he wants to devour you. And today when you fell, he couldn't get to you fast enough."

"He was so angry."

Laurel smiled. "No, he was afraid that you were hurt."

Suddenly a funny feeling settled in Brooke's stomach. Trent was worried about her?

"Seriously, you need to pay attention," Laurel said shaking her head. "I wonder how many good guys you let get away?"

They both laughed, then Laurel suddenly hugged Brooke. "I know Mom and Dad are upset you're here, but I'm glad you came to find me." Laurel pulled back. "It's crazy, isn't it? You're my sister."

Brooke didn't expect to feel these emotions, but then she realized it wasn't only her and Coralee anymore, now she had Laurel, too. Of course that didn't stop the longing for the two men she couldn't have in her life.

THAT EVENING AFTER a long shower, Trent dressed in an old army T-shirt and a pair of sweatpants. He came downstairs barefoot and dropped into his dad's overstuffed chair. He wasn't moving from this spot for the next few hours, then he'd head back to the cabin. The hot spray had helped his sore shoulders, but he had another day of roundup. They'd gotten Rory's branding done, and tomorrow it was his turn. He was glad that his herd was smaller.

He'd made sure that his ranch hands were ready for tomorrow. Ricky promised an early night, and he'd have the horses saddled and ready by dawn.

His thoughts turned to Brooke. It was difficult leaving her alone today, especially after her tumble off Raven. She had to be sore. He thought about inviting her to use the Jacuzzi, but immediately nixed the idea. She'd be too tempting. He hoped she'd gone back at the cabin at least, and was in bed. He groaned. He didn't need to think about her there, either, not if he wanted any sleep tonight.

His cell rang. Seeing the ID, he wasn't sure if he wanted to answer tonight. Finally he pressed the button and said, "Hey, Swamp Man, it's about time you called me."

"I texted you," Cody said. "But I had to go back out on surveillance, and I only have a few minutes now to talk, so here's the scoop. I finished your reports on Coralee and Brooke Harper. The info isn't bad, but you might find the facts interesting. Also, my guy found out a little more on Aldrich. Not much, but maybe enough to help in the search to find him."

Trent wasn't as interested in the runaway contractor as he was in Brooke. "I can't thank you enough, Cody."

"Not a problem, Rocky. How do you want it? Email okay?"

"Sounds great. Send it my way."

"Okay, you got it. Talk to you later, Rocky."

"Thanks, Swamp Man."

Pocketing his phone, Trent got out of the chair and headed to retrieve another beer from the refrigerator. He took a drink as he passed the doors leading to the deck and the empty Jacuzzi. He immediately thought of the night he'd spent with Brooke. He closed his eyes and re-lived the feel of holding her, touching her heated skin. His body tensed with desire. He'd never wanted a woman this badly. If Rory hadn't burst in on them, would they have made love? He shook those wayward thoughts from his head and walked back to the office.

He was anxious to say the least as he brought up his emails and opened the file. He wasn't sure what he'd find out on Brooke, but he had to read it. He pushed Print and sat back.

Suddenly there was a knock at the door. He glanced at the clock to see it was eight o'clock. He guessed it was probably one of his men. He got up and walked through the kitchen to the back door. The porch light showed the small silhouette of Brooke.

Pulse pounding, he opened the door and motioned for her to come inside. "Brooke, what are you doing here?

Silently she walked past him, and he inhaled that soft citrus scent of her hair. She had on the long skirt and sweater from the other night. She mesmerized him with those big eyes. She bit down on her lower lip nervously. "I came to see you."

She hesitated, and swallowed hard. "Do you still want me?"

Chapter Fourteen

Brooke couldn't breathe. How was she supposed to seduce this man if she couldn't draw air into her lungs? Instead she grabbed the front of his shirt and pulled him down to meet her gaze.

"I asked, do you still want me, Trent Landry?"

His eyes darkened to a rich chocolate, and she was getting hungrier waiting for him to decide. Luckily she didn't have to wait long.

"Yes. Hell, yes, I want you. But you better be damn sure this is what you want, too."

She wanted this night with him so badly she pushed her fear aside. "I'm sure."

Trent released a sigh. His hands cupped her face as the pad of his thumb touched her lower lip, then brushed back and forth. "This mouth of yours has been driving me crazy since I met you."

"Only my mouth?" she asked bravely. Where did that come from?

His breath mingled with hers and her pulse quickened. He rewarded her with a cocky smile and he moved closer. "Do you want me to name all the other parts, or just show you?"

He brushed his mouth against hers and there was a

faint taste of beer. She was the one getting intoxicated. "Show me," she whispered.

He rewarded her when he leaned down and nipped at her lips, letting his nose drag against hers. Her eyes drifted shut as he kissed her again. This time, his tongue moved along her lips, then dipped inside, causing an erotic friction she'd never experienced before. She'd never experienced a lot of things, and hoped Trent would show her what she'd been missing.

Trent's arms tightened around her waist, bringing her against his arousal. She whimpered, and his tongue delved inside once again. Another shudder ran through her and she moaned softly.

He pulled back. "I don't know why you showed up at my door, but damn, I'm glad you're here."

She linked her arms around his neck. "Good. I was beginning to wonder if you were upset that I just showed up."

"Babe, don't ever doubt that I want you. I want you anywhere I can have you." He reached down and swung her up into his arms. "I better keep my promise to let you know how glad I am you stopped by."

Trent somehow managed to carry her through the house and up the stairs to his room.

"No one has ever carried me before…you," she whispered against his ear as her arms wrapped around his neck. "Only you." Her soft hair tickled, raising his desire a notch higher.

He kicked open the bedroom door and crossed the carpeted floor to the king-size bed. He sucked in a breath as he lowered her to the floor, feeling every one of her luscious curves sliding against him. Once she was standing, he took her mouth in another heated kiss. Then another, and they were both breathless.

"You're wearing too much for what I have in mind."

Filtered light came into the room from the hallway, making the space seem more intimate. That was enough for now, but he swore that soon, he would see her in the morning light. He took the edge of her sweater and pulled it off over her head and tossed it aside. His gaze met hers. He searched for any doubt, but only found desire in those incredible emerald depths.

He touched her through her lace bra and sampled the weight in his palms. "You are beautiful, Brooke."

She closed her eyes and gasped. "That feels…wonderful."

Her praise spurred him on and he unlatched the clasp, allowing her breasts to spill out. "Let's see if I can do better than wonderful."

Her fingers gripped his arms. "Oh, Trent…"

He took her mouth again in another searing kiss. His hands went to her skirt and tugged it down over her hips, then he slipped off her short boots. He stood and took the time to examine her dressed in only a pair of panties.

He wanted to yank those off, too. Instead, he removed his T-shirt, and pulled her against his body as his mouth came down and captured hers. The kiss nearly consumed him. Still it wasn't enough, he had to have all of her. "I want you, Brooke."

"I want you, too. Make love to me. Please."

"Darlin', I plan to." He guided her to sit down on the bed. He covered her mouth with his, pressing her back onto the mattress and came down beside her. He raised himself up and looked at her. "Tell me you're sure, Brooke. We can stop if you…" *It would kill me.* "I don't want you to have any regrets."

Her hand touched his face and he turned, placing a tender kiss against her palm.

"I would never regret making love with you, Trent. I want you."

Brooke trembled. Her body stirred with a need she'd never known before. She wanted to experience this with Trent. She couldn't bear it if he wanted to stop. She reached up to meet his kiss, and wrapped her arms around him to keep him close.

He kissed her again and his touch was incredible but she needed more.

Suddenly, a sensation caused her to gasp. Her hands slid over his bare back, feeling the muscles ripple against her fingers, then she dug her nails into his flesh when the pleasure grew out of control. "Trent…"

"Give me a second," Trent said as he got off the bed and stripped out of his pants. He reached into the drawer and took out a foil packet. After taking care of protection, he came back to her… She could only manage to moan at the sheer pleasure of their joining. They needed to talk about what just happened here. At the moment, though, he couldn't seem to let go of Brooke. He rubbed her arm, cradling her body against his chest.

"Seems you neglected to tell me a few things before your seduction," he said.

When Brooke remained silent, he cupped her cheek and made her look at him. "Why didn't you tell me that you never…that this was your first time?"

She shrugged. "For exactly this reason. When you get to a certain age, you're expected to have experience. I just never had much of a chance to date, and after my mother…" She sighed. "She'd made too many bad choices in men, and I didn't want to go down that path." Her gaze met his. "Most people just took for granted I already had."

Something squeezed around his heart. "Like Rory?"

Her eyes widened. "I can't blame him. My mother hadn't been truthful with him. But I wouldn't have come here if not for my mother."

Trent realized his life would be less complicated if Brooke hadn't come to Colorado. But he sure was very glad she was here. "Still, you should have waited to give yourself to your future husband." Suddenly he hated the thought of another man touching her.

"I guess, but that's a long way off."

Her eyes were so incredibly beautiful, so full of wonder. How had she survived working in Las Vegas and remained so innocent?

"I wanted it to be you," she whispered.

He was touched beyond words, but he couldn't let her think there could be more. "I'm an ex-soldier, Brooke. I'm set in my ways and I work eighteen-hour days trying to rebuild this ranch. That's my focus. I have nothing to offer you."

"Did I ask you for anything?" Covering her nakedness with the sheet, Brooke sat up. "I only wanted tonight, okay. Maybe experience what it was like to be with a cowboy." She tried to climb off the bed, but he pulled her back and his mouth covered hers.

He ended the kiss, but didn't pull away. "Don't cheapen what happened between us." He could feel every curve, and now that he'd sampled her, he wasn't sure he could walk away.

He saw tears flood her eyes. She nodded.

"God, Brooke, you make me crazy. You make me wish things could be different." His hand moved up and down her arm. "I've never wanted a woman as much as I want you."

"Stop, Trent. I told you, I don't need promises. You've given me more tonight than I ever dreamed of. Making love with you was a beautiful experience. Thank you." She glanced away. "Maybe I should go back to the cabin."

Maybe that was a good idea, but he didn't like it. He got out of bed and walked into the bathroom across the hall. Damn, what had he done? Why did he keep reaching for things he couldn't have? Like a brother who would never be able to grow up, and a husband and wife who would never be a happy family ever again. Now Brooke Harper was right on the top of that list.

BROOKE WASN'T GOING to cry. She got out of bed and hurried to get dressed. If she were lucky, she could get out of the house before Trent returned. Well, she'd handled that well. *Thanks, Laurel, for your advice. Go after what you want*, Laurel had said.

Face it, she might have been good enough to warm Trent Landry's bed for one night, but he wasn't about to declare his undying love. Thank the Lord, she hadn't blurted out any declaration, either.

Now, she was trying to find a way to make a graceful exit. She pulled her sweater over her head and stepped into her skirt. After slipping on her boots, she went to the dresser and looked in the mirror. She ran her fingers through her hair, and started to leave when she saw the stack of bundled envelopes on the dresser.

She couldn't stop herself and picked them up. They were all addressed to Sergeant Major Trent W. Landry U.S. Army from Wade Landry. There had to be a dozen letters there.

"Find anything interesting?"

She jumped at the sound of the familiar voice and looked up to see Trent. He'd put on a pair of boxers. "Oh, sorry, Trent." She put down the letters. "I didn't mean to snoop. I mean…they were just there." She stopped. "I apologize again."

Trent leaned against the door frame and folded his arms

so he wouldn't touch her. To stay angry was the best de-
fense. "No, I'm the one who should apologize. They're
letters my father sent me while I was overseas. I guess
I'm touchy because he died before I made it home. I just
couldn't read the last ones that arrived after his death."
Why was he always spilling his guts to this woman? "Honestly, I'm ashamed that I hadn't visited him in a long
time."

"Did your dad know you felt guilty about Chris?"

He blinked. "You don't know how I feel."

She went to him and placed her hand against his heart.
"What happened that day, Trent?"

He shook his head. "Talking won't help bring Chris
back."

"It might help you forgive yourself. You were only a
child back then, too. Why do you feel your brother's death
was your fault?"

"You don't understand. If I had taken Chris riding with
me that day, then he'd be alive now."

Brooke tried to hide her shock at Trent's declaration,
but she couldn't pull it off. She wanted to hold him, help
share his burden, but she felt him tense. "What happened,
Trent?"

He grabbed his jeans from the floor and pulled them
on. She thought he was going to dismiss her question,
then he sank down on the edge of the bed. He hung his
head and studied the carpet. She was having none of that
and knelt down in front of him, praying he wouldn't turn
her away.

"I was thirteen and my friend Josh had come to spend
the night. Chris tried his best to horn in on our time.
I kept telling him to go away. Of course, being nine
years old, he was persistent. The next morning, Josh

and I decided we'd head out early for our ride and ditch Chris."

Brooke squeezed his hands. "There's nothing terrible about you wanting to be with your friend."

Trent swallowed. "What I should have realized was that Chris would try and come after us. For only being nine, he was a good rider and wanted to do everything I did. I have no doubt he would have followed after Dad and gone on the rodeo circuit." He blinked a few times. "Josh and I were headed to Rainbow Canyon and planned to spend the day. There were some wild horses around there and we got this crazy idea to try and rope them."

Brooke got a glimpse of a boyish grin before it disappeared. "A sudden storm moved in and we had to head home. That's when we found out Chris was missing. Mom and Dad thought he was with us. Then his horse showed up without him. They called in a search party…and that night they found him at the bottom of a ravine."

Brooke's heart was breaking. For the boy who died too young, and the man who'd carried the guilt all his life. "I'm sorry, Trent. Sorry this awful accident happened to a young boy. But you're not to blame. And I don't think Chris would want you to, either."

Trent didn't say a word.

"You know another thing, I have no doubt Chris thought you were the best brother. Why would he want to be with you all the time?"

Trent's gaze met hers and she could find so much to love about this man. Of course he wasn't ready to hear any of it. "So forgive yourself."

He knew he was getting too close to Brooke, but he couldn't seem to stop himself. He leaned forward and pressed a tender kiss against her sweet mouth. He wanted to pull her into his arms and bury himself deep inside her once again. "Thank you. You've helped me more than you know."

Brooke burrowed deeper against his chest. "You're welcome."

Everyone needed love and acceptance, and that included Brooke. She came here to help her mother, but was there more to her story? "What else brought you to the Bucking Q?"

"Why do you think there's more?"

He pulled back and looked at her. "I'm going to be honest with you. My friend Cody Marsh, the PI, sent his report to me right before you showed up at my door."

She didn't hide her panicked look.

"Why don't we have a look at it together?" He took her hand, then they walked down the stairs and to the office in the back of the house.

"Trent, we don't need to do this tonight."

"We do, because Rory will want to know about your mother. And tomorrow, we have another roundup."

He had her sit in the chair and he went to the printer. He picked up the papers from the report.

Trent leaned on the edge of the desk. "When Rory found out you were here, he asked me to have a PI investigate you and Coralee. Cody Marsh and I were in the army together. I trust him to be honest and thorough."

Brooke's eyes widened, and he could see the pulse beating in her neck. "What did he find?"

He handed her the report. "You tell me, Brooke." He wanted her to trust him enough to tell him everything. "I haven't seen it yet."

She glanced down at the papers. "It will tell you what I already have, my job at the casino, my address where I live. That my mother is in the Carlton Care Facility with Alzheimer's and she's rapidly losing her grasp on reality. I haven't done anything wrong and I'm not wanted for any crimes."

"But you left something out."

She glanced away, then back at him. "Yes, I did."

He was almost afraid to find out the answer. "Then trust me enough to tell me."

She sat up straighter. "Laurel isn't my half sister. She's my twin sister."

All right, maybe that did surprise him. Then he realized what that meant. "You're Rory's daughter?"

She handed him back the report. "See for yourself. My date of birth is the same as Laurel's."

He began to read the information. Twin daughters, Laurel Kathryn and Brooke Marie were born to Coralee Harper in September nineteen hundred and eighty-eight in a hospital outside Atlanta, Georgia. It was the same town Coralee's parents called home.

Trent looked at Brooke. He wanted to reach for her and hold her. "Then why in the hell did you say you were Laurel's half sister?"

"Because when I arrived, the Quinns weren't home. And you were a stranger to me. I didn't know much about Rory Quinn, either. My promise to my mother was to bring Laurel to see her. It wasn't my plan to search for my father."

He didn't believe that. He leaned forward and gripped her hands. They were cold and clammy. "You can't say you weren't curious about him."

"Whether I was or wasn't doesn't matter. Rory Quinn wasn't crazy about finding me here."

She held up a hand before he could talk. "It's not Rory's fault. I don't blame him for hating Coralee. She used him, like she'd used a lot of men." She blinked back tears. "He

has his daughter Laurel. He doesn't need me around reminding him of his past."

Trent was frustrated, and he hurt for Brooke. Damn
the woman, Coralee Harper sure had done a number on
her daughter. "Look, Brooke, I've gotten to know you in
the past few days."

"No kidding."

He couldn't help a smile. He also wished he could take
her back to bed and make her forget the rest of the world's
problems.

"I know Rory hasn't exactly been warm toward you.
But you have to give him a chance. Not just for you, but
for a future relationship between you and Laurel. You two
look so much alike that it's only a matter of time before
someone figures it out."

Brooke stood and walked across the room. She hadn't
meant for her secret to come out. Not like this. "The last
thing I want is to cause any more trouble for the family.
I only want to spend a few days with my sister. If Laurel
decides to come back to Las Vegas that would be great,
but I won't force myself into the Quinns' life. And no matter what Coralee has done in the past, she's my mother,
and she's sick and has no one but me." *And I have no one
but her*, she added silently.

"I get that, but Rory deserves to know who you are. If
you don't tell him and he finds out, it'll break the man's
heart."

Then they'd have a matching set, because Brooke's
heart was already broken. Not just because she couldn't
have her father in her life, but because she couldn't have
Trent.

AN HOUR LATER, Brooke turned down Trent's invitation
for supper. She wanted to be alone, to try to figure out

what to do. Even with her arguing that she could get back to the cabin without Trent following, she lost the battle.

Once out of her car, he walked her to the porch, waited patiently as she unlocked the door, but when she turned around, he pulled her into his arms.

"Call me crazy, but I need another taste of you, and the feel of your body against mine." His mouth captured hers in a hungry kiss. She wrapped her arms around his neck and took what he offered. It was as if they both knew their time was quickly running out. She wanted some memories to take away with her. He finally broke off the kiss and pressed his forehead against hers.

"I better get out of here. We've got a roundup at dawn."

"Do I still get to go along?" She prayed he wouldn't take that away from her. "I mean, I won't do anything crazy and fall off my horse."

Trent squeezed her tight. "You better come along." He wasn't ready to give her up, either. "There's a barbecue tomorrow night to celebrate the end of the roundup."

"I won't intrude on the party. I'll just come back here." She forced a smile. "I'll probably be sore from the ride."

"No, you earned it. You've worked so hard."

She glanced away. "Trent, you don't have to do that. I know the Quinns will have friends there…they'll have questions."

"Dammit, I know I don't have to. I want you there with me." His mouth crushed down on hers. By the time he broke away, they were breathing hard. "I want you so badly my eyes are crossing. The only thing that is keeping me from carrying you inside and into your bed is the fact that we will be getting up in a few hours. So good night, Brooke."

He pushed her inside and closed the door and walked over to his solitary cabin. He better get used to it, because once Brooke left, he would be alone once again.

Chapter Fifteen

The morning had come too soon, especially when Trent hadn't gotten much sleep. He'd been kept awake for hours, thinking about Brooke.

How would he ever be able to forget that look on her pretty face when she walked through his back door? The soft, breathy sounds she'd made when he'd touched her… made love to her.

Now, two hours sitting in the saddle with cattle bawling all around, the sun pounding against his back, he still couldn't get her out of his head. He stole a glance over his shoulder to see her trailing the herd. Forgetting her might be easier if she weren't so close.

He hadn't been able to concentrate much since Brooke walked into his life. Since he'd let her get close. It hadn't been so long since he'd felt the need to confide in anyone. He'd spent most of his adult life trying to keep people at a distance. The only exception was the Quinns.

Now, he knew a secret that could rock their world even more. How would this end up, good or bad? Would Brooke end up getting hurt? Would Rory accept her? His chest ached for all the people who were important to him.

"Hey, boss."

He turned as Ricky rode up next to him. "There are a few strays back in the canyon." He pointed off to the west. "I was wondering if I could take Brooke along to gather them up. I thought she might get a kick out of it."

He looked back to see Brooke coming toward him. She'd been riding drag all morning without complaint, so why not? Then he considered the rougher terrain and her inexperience. He felt panic stir in his gut as he thought about Chris…the accident.

"How many are there?"

Ricky shrugged. "Maybe four or five."

"Then take Mike with you. The territory around there isn't for a beginner."

If Ricky disagreed with his decision, he didn't say. "Sure." The kid wheeled his horse around and took off, calling to Mike to join him.

Trent shifted his horse sideways so Brooke could ride beside him.

"I can't go?" she asked.

He shook his head, trying to see how she was today. She hadn't spoken much earlier when they saddled up their mounts. Last night had been incredible, but today, reality intervened along with all the unresolved issues between them. That didn't mean he didn't care about her. Maybe too much.

"It's too dangerous, Brooke. The terrain is rocky and the ground isn't stable. You aren't experienced enough to handle a horse that might dump you."

She sent him a challenging look. "I handled it just fine yesterday."

"And you were thrown." He leaned toward her. "I don't want to see you get hurt, Brooke. Seeing you lying on the ground yesterday about killed me."

She blushed. "I'm sorry. I'm not used to people being so protective."

Reaching out, he covered her hand with his. "Get

used to it." He didn't know how to handle his feelings for her. Last night in bed with Brooke should have been a no-strings fling, but it sure didn't turn out that way. "Stay with the herd, Brooke, or go back to the cabin. Your choice." He kicked his heels into Rango's sides and rode off.

Brooke wasn't sure what she'd done to cause his anger. She looked around at several other riders helping out today. She really wasn't needed, but she hated to think about not being on horseback. It was probably her last time.

Laurel came up beside her. "Seems you have a way of riling that man. What did you do this time?"

"He doesn't want me to go after strays with Ricky."

Laurel tugged on her hat. "My, my, the man is very protective of you. Also the fact that this area is a little rougher."

Brooke grew serious. "Maybe he's thinking about Chris."

Laurel shot her a quick look. "So he told you about his brother's accident, huh?"

"Some," she admitted.

Laurel nodded. "It was tragic for all of us, but especially for Trent. They were really close. Chris was a year older than me, but we were friends." She released a breath as if to bring herself back from her reverie. "I better get back to work. I need to relieve Chet." She took off toward the rear of the herd. Brooke glanced around, and decided to stay where she was. The Lucky Bar L's herd was smaller than yesterday's so she could enjoy the nice day.

"How are you doing today?" She turned to find Rory had ridden up beside her.

Don't be nervous, she told herself. "I'm fine. It's a nice day." Darn, she didn't know what to say to this man.

He adjusted his brown cowboy hat. "Any effects from your tumble yesterday?"

"I'm a little sore, but not enough to keep me away today. Probably my last time ever doing a roundup."

Rory nodded in Laurel's direction. "Not if my daughter has anything to say about it. She let both Diane and me know that she wants to spend time with you."

A huge ache pulled in Brooke's chest. She was becoming pretty fond of Laurel, too.

"I'd like that, but please believe me, I don't want to cause any trouble for your family." Maybe she should just give Rory the PI's report and let him read the truth.

"I think you two girls can work something out."

"So you're okay with us spending time together?"

She watched the older man handle his large horse. He sat tall in the saddle, and he held the reins loosely. Yet, he had total command of the large animal. Something inside her wanted to shout like a little girl, "Hey, this is my dad."

"Laurel's an adult," Rory said. "She makes her own choices."

"Thank you, Mr. Quinn. I promise, I won't do anything to hurt Laurel. It's just nice to have…some family."

Rory studied her a moment, then stared off at the trail. "I guess that's not too much to ask." He smiled and rode back to his position.

Brooke felt a flicker of hope. Maybe the man didn't hate her.

The rest of the afternoon went pretty fast. When the last of the herd had been branded, tagged and inoculated, they called the roundup a success.

Rory drew everyone's attention when he invited the crew and the neighbors back to the house for a barbecue. Being with everyone tonight could be wonderful. It was probably her last night here in Colorado, and she wanted to spend it with the three people she'd come to love.

AT SIX O'CLOCK, the barbecue was in full swing. Trent had come by early to help out, but thanks to Diane and some of the other ranchers' wives, things were nearly ready.

There was quite an assortment of side dishes lining the serving table, and that didn't include the several cuts of beef that had been cooking all day in the smoker. There would be more than enough food for everyone.

Paper lanterns were strung over several tables covered in white paper awaiting the guests: friends, neighbors and ranch hands. Even a DJ was setting up for entertainment and dancing later, in the concrete driveway.

Trent looked around, but he didn't see Brooke anywhere. Darn, if she didn't show up soon, he was going to find her. He wanted to bring her tonight, but she insisted on meeting him here. He should be happy she wasn't the clingy type. Then why did he hate that it felt as if she was pulling away?

Over the past week, they'd spent so much time together, then last night, he'd made love to her, getting a taste of something he'd never felt with a woman before. Yet, her secret put another barrier between them. She had to go to Rory.

He suddenly heard the familiar laughter, and turned to find Brooke standing with Chet and Ricky. His breath caught as his gaze traveled over her. She had on a soft red sweater belted at the waist. A long black skirt showed off her shapely hips.

The late September evening was chilly, but the heaters and fire ring kept the area warm. He walked over to the group as she turned around.

She smiled. "Trent."

He wanted to lean in and steal a kiss, and brand her to let everyone know she was his. Whoa, where did that come from?

He took her by the arm and walked her away from the group into a more private area. "You look nice, Brooke." His gaze locked on her pretty face. "I'm glad you decided to come."

"Laurel said I shouldn't miss tonight. It was going to be a lot of fun."

He leaned forward and murmured, "I can think of a lot of fun things to do with you."

She blushed. "Trent…"

"I want to spend this evening with you, Brooke."

"Okay, I'm here, Trent. I don't want people to think…"

After last night, everything had changed between them. They'd shared more than just her first time making love. They'd shared secrets, fears and sadness. And he wanted to spend as much time with her as possible. "That you're trying to push your way into the Quinns' life."

She glanced away and nodded.

"How about we get something to eat and enjoy this time together?"

Trent took her by the hand and they went to the food line. He introduced her to some of the neighbors who came tonight. Heaped high with samples of all the dishes, they brought the plates back to a table, where Chet and Laurel were seated. They were talking horses, of course.

Brooke sat down across from her sister, and they fell into an easy conversation as if they'd known each other a long time. Was that the twin connection thing? Even being separated for years, they still seemed to have a bond. He could imagine how much closer they'd be if Brooke told Laurel the truth.

Laurel looked at Trent. "Can you talk Brooke out of

leaving tomorrow? I said she's more than welcome to stay until Sunday."

Trent stopped his fork's journey to his mouth and looked at Brooke. "You're leaving tomorrow?"

She shrugged. "I probably should. I can pick up a work shift on Sunday."

Laurel beamed. "Isn't it cool my sister is a card dealer?"

Brooke laughed. "And my sister is a horse trainer."

"If you stay, I can give you more riding lessons," Laurel said.

"You better take her up on that. Laurel's private lessons are expensive."

They all turned to see Rory standing beside the table, then he sat down in the vacant spot next to his daughter. "This gal is the best at what she does."

Brooke's heart raced. He wanted her to stay. "I've intruded far too long as it is."

"You're not intruding," Rory said. "The cabin isn't rented yet. The place would only sit empty if you left."

"Thank you for the offer, Mr. Quinn."

Rory's expression softened. "I think you can call me Rory."

Brooke nodded, and her voice trembled a little when she spoke. "Thank you, Rory. Your offer is generous. I appreciate it more than you know."

Rory looked at Trent. "Will you be ready to ship the cows on Monday?"

"Yes, I have the cattle haulers and drivers lined up for the first thing that morning." At least he had something to do to distract him from Brooke's departure.

"Then we can concentrate on finishing the cabins," Rory said as he looked at Brooke again. "I might want to hear a little about your ideas on us advertising for weddings."

She felt her heart swell. "I could send you some brochures on the hotel's services. You could downsize whatever you can't do." She glanced at Trent, then back to
Rory. "I know it's important to get your cabins to start
making revenue, and weddings is a good way."

"Laurel said something about starting out focusing
on New Year's Eve and Valentine's Day and some of the
summer holidays."

Another thrill rushed through Brooke. "I can show
you how to expand your website to include that venue."

He nodded, then began eating his food. It wasn't much,
but Rory had reached out to her. She looked at Trent and
he winked at her. Suddenly she was hungry.

Thirty minutes later, the DJ opened the party with
some music. As George Strait filled the air, Brooke enjoyed sharing conversation with her sister and father.
They'd joked about some of the antics of the past two
days. She was overjoyed that she'd been included in the
roundup. She could go home with those memories.

Diane had come to sit on the other side of her husband,
but she never acknowledged that Brooke was there. That
was okay. She was a threat to her family, and she understood that. That was a big reason Brooke didn't want tell
Rory all the truth. It would hurt Diane, and maybe their
marriage.

She couldn't cause them more trouble, not the way her
mother had done years ago. She wouldn't do that to them.
No matter how much she wanted to be part of this family.

Trent looked at Rory. "I think it's time to start the an-
nouncements."

Rory nodded, and both men got up from the table,
went to the DJ stand and borrowed his microphone. The
music died away.

Rory went first. "Welcome, friends and neighbors," he

began. "First of all, we want to thank you all for your help these past two days. Even our men, who get paid to do this kind of work, went that extra mile for the Bucking Q and the Lucky Bar L ranches. Our success is measured by the quality of people who work for us. Thank you, guys."

The ranch hands cheered and whistled, then Rory's men began to chant *Bucking Q*, while Trent's men chanted *Lucky Bar L*.

Both Rory and Trent grinned, enjoying the camaraderie they had with their employees.

Trent finally raised a hand to quiet the crowd. "Like every year, at roundup we hand out some special awards," he said. The crowd cheered as Laurel came up front carrying a box.

Trent spoke into the microphone. "Seems our men like to compete." A cheer rose through the group. "Our first challenge is for the fastest man to bring a calf to the ground. This year the award goes to Mike from the Lucky Bar L." Everyone cheered as the shy man went up to get his trophy and an envelope with some cash.

"Good job, Mike," Trent said. "Next is the wrangler who's the fastest chasing down strays, also from the Lucky Bar L, Ricky Pierson."

Ricky jumped up with a fist pump in the air. Someone in the crowd called out, "He's pretty fast with the ladies, too."

Laughter rang out as Ricky accepted his trophy and cash, then held it overhead.

The next two awards went to Chet and Larry from the Bucking Q for team roping. Then Rory took the microphone from Trent and looked out in the crowd. "This last award goes to our most improved wrangler. She rode drag through most of the two-day roundup, without any complaints. She also took a pretty big spill off her horse, but got right back on, and kept going. This year's Best Rookie Wrangler goes to Brooke Harper."

Feeling shaky, Brooke saw Laurel wave for her to come up. She finally stood as the ranch hands cheered and whistled for her. Blushing, she accepted the trophy from Laurel and held it high, then went back to her seat.

Trent winked at her, then spoke to the crowd. "Now, everyone stick around and enjoy the music." He headed back to the table and sat down beside her.

"Did you have something to do with this?" she asked him.

Trent shook his head. "No, we hand out trophies every year. You know guys, we like everything to be a competition, including a best new guy award. Laurel won it on her first roundup, too."

"How old was she, ten?"

Trent grinned. "I think eight."

Brooke kept staring down at the silly plastic trophy of a horse. Why did it mean so much to her? This was crazy. It was just a silly award.

Another song began, Alabama's "Forever's As Far As I'll Go." Trent reached for her hand. "Let's dance."

She shook her head. "I don't know how," she told him.

"Then it's time you learned," he said. "I'll teach you." Taking her hand, he led her to the floor, then pulled her into his arms. "It's slow so we'll work on a little country waltz. This also has benefits, because I get to hold you close."

Brooke felt his body shift closer against hers, and the contact sent a shiver through her as rich baritone voices filled her head. She loved being in Trent's arms. Memories of last night came flooding back. The feel of his tender touch, his mouth traveling over her body, his slow easy loving…

Trent's voice broke through her reverie. "You were a good sport accepting the trophy."

Trent's heart tripped when Brooke looked up at him and smiled.

"Are you kidding?" she said. "I've never won anything before. That trophy is going in a special place of honor."

He kissed the end of her nose, then drew her back and pressed his chin to her forehead.

Trent shut his eyes, wondering why he was torturing himself. And Brooke in his arms, gave him ideas he didn't need, especially with the PI report looming over them.

Last night, he'd read over the three pages after he dropped off Brooke. Outside of her birth date, everything she told him had been true. Cody's report also stated her address in Las Vegas. A side note from his friend stated it wasn't a favorable part of town.

Now that her mother was in a nursing home, maybe Brooke could move into a nicer neighborhood. Surely her new job would pay better enabling her to relocate to a safer place.

He pulled her closer. He inhaled her powdery scent as he listened to the words of the song. "Forever's as far as I'll go…" He breathed a sigh. If only he still believed in forever.

THE PARTY FINALLY broke up about ten o'clock. Brooke said goodbye to the neighbors she'd met tonight but knew she'd probably never see again.

She enjoyed herself, and spending time with Laurel and Rory had been the best part. When Rory hadn't been visiting with his guests, he came back to her table where he and Laurel spent time with her.

Trent had danced with her a few more times, and as

much as she loved being in his arms, this was his night to play cohost with Rory.

Most of the women had cleaned up during the event, so Brooke only found a few paper plates and cups and dumped them into the trash. The food had been wrapped up and taken inside the kitchen. That was a good thing because she didn't want to intrude on Diane Quinn any longer. She knew Laurel's mother was upset about her being here.

She was gathering her purse and sweater when Rory called to her.

"I was just going to find you to say good-night and thank you for inviting me tonight," Brooke said.

"You're welcome." He paused and she got worried. "If you're going to be around tomorrow could you stop by the house?"

She swallowed back her fear. Had he discovered the truth? "Of course."

"Don't look so worried. I wanted to talk to you about the website and some ideas about our advertising. It's no secret that we need to make some money and fast."

She was thrilled. "Of course, I'll help in any way I can."

He tipped his hat. "Thank you, I appreciate the help. Stop by when it's convenient. Good night."

"Good night, Rory."

She just stood there and watched the man walk away.

Trent came up to her. "You ready to head back to the cabin?"

Still flying high on adrenaline, she hated to see this evening end. "You stay with your friends. Chet can walk me back there."

He frowned. "Are you trying to get rid of me?"

She shook her head. "No, of course not. I just thought that you would want to stay and visit with your friends."

With little effort, he pulled her close and nuzzled her neck. "My friends have all gone home. These older guys are friends of the Quinns, and if I stay I'll have to hear about the old glory days, riding the rodeo circuit."

She arched her neck allowing his mouth to have access to that sensitive spot below her ear. She was quickly turning to mush. Then she realized there were people around. "Stop, people will see us."

"Hold that thought." He crossed the yard to the group of men talking with Rory. He said something to the older man, then shook hands with the group, and walked back to her.

Her pulse raced, seeing the determined look on the handsome cowboy's face. As he got closer, she could see the heat in his gaze. She swallowed, recalling last night in his bed.

"Come on. I want you all to myself." He grabbed her hand, headed to the truck and lifted her inside. The short drive to the cabins was silent. When he pulled up to her door, he climbed out and went to her side and she willingly went into his arms.

Trent wasn't sure what he was doing, except he couldn't let Brooke go. He wanted her. He carried her to the porch and managed to get the key into the lock, then the door swung open.

Once inside, he kicked the door shut, but didn't move from his spot. He didn't want to think about the secrets, or Rory or Laurel or Coralee. Tonight, he wanted to be with this woman.

"I want you, Brooke Harper. I want to spend the night making love to you. If you have a problem with that then you better tell me now."

She inhaled sharply, then leaned in and brushed a kiss on his mouth. "Not a one."

He continued down the hall and into the bedroom. He set her down and breathed a kiss over her lips, but backed away before he lost it totally.

He unhooked her belt and let it drop to the floor. "I've wanted you since you appeared at the party." He pulled the sweater off over her head, leaving her in a lacy bra. "I hope you feel the same."

"I do." Her heaving breath nearly had her breasts spilling out.

Trent's mouth covered hers in a hungry kiss, but soon his lips began trailing a path along her heated skin to her breasts. With a groan, he pulled back, popped the snaps on his Western shirt, and stripped the fabric off his shoulders and arms, then tossed it aside. Then he reached for her bra and removed that, as well.

Brooke's hand shook as she reached out to press her fingertips to his chest. She shivered, feeling the heat of his bare skin. He sucked in a breath and she pulled back.

He took her hand and flattened her palm against his flesh. "I love your hands on me."

Feeling brave, she stepped closer and pressed a kiss against his nipple.

"Oh, babe, now you're playing with fire."

She liked a challenge. She continued the kisses until he'd had enough and quickly tugged off her skirt and boots, and sat her down on the bed. Then he worked off his boots and jeans, and placing a knee on the mattress, he leaned over her.

Brooke placed her finger over his lips. "Don't talk. Showing me is better." Just for a little while she wanted to pretend she could love this man.

Trent leaned down and his mouth covered hers, and her fantasy began.

Chapter Sixteen

The next morning, Trent got up at 5:00 a.m, but only to go into the other room to call Ricky and give him the list of chores for the day. It had been a while since he'd taken any time off, but this morning he was making an exception.

He tossed his phone on the counter, walked into the dark bedroom and climbed in bed beside the sleeping Brooke. Slipping under the covers, he pressed against her warm body, she automatically turned and curled into him. Her arm rested on his chest.

He felt his body rouse, which seemed impossible after spending most of the night loving this beautiful woman. He'd never been with anyone that made him feel so... He couldn't even find the words. Brooke's innocence had touched him, humbled him, making him want to be a better lover, a better man.

"Trent," she murmured against his chest and her hand began to move.

He covered hers with his. "I'm here, babe."

She raised her head. "Don't you have to go feed the stock?" Her voice was low and sultry in the darkness.

He kissed her nose. "No, I took the day off. I plan to spend it here with you. Whatever you want to do."

She moaned. "Sleep."

"Really, you want to sleep the day away?"

She brushed back her messy hair and rested her chin on his chest and blinked those pretty eyes at him. "Unless you have a better idea."

He groaned. "I created a monster."

"I don't recall you complaining last night…or this morning."

He pushed her onto her back and leaned over her. Every curve of her body was pressed against his, making him want her again. "As wonderful as that invitation is, I thought I would take you into town for some breakfast."

"Now? The sun isn't even up, yet."

"Welcome to ranch life." He didn't want to remind her that her hometown of Las Vegas never sleeps.

Her gaze met his as her hands cupped his face. "It's a nice life you have here, Trent. Quiet and serene, with nice neighbors. And horses you can ride anytime."

"Glad you like it." He brushed a soft kiss on her lips. "That means you'll come back here and visit me."

He felt her tense. "It will be a while before I have any time off. And Coralee will probably have a fit if I leave her again."

He had no idea how far Coralee's disease had progressed, but most Alzheimer's patients that he'd heard about seemed to lose their memory pretty quickly.

"So Coralee still recognizes you?"

Brooke paused. "Not always. She goes in and out of reality. That's how I learned about Laurel. She started calling me by her name."

"I'm sorry, Brooke. It has to be difficult to stand by and see this happening to her."

She glanced away. "I have a good support team with Erin. I never would have been able to come here without her help."

"I, for one, am very glad you came here. And Coralee is lucky to have you."

She kissed him. "Thank you."

"You're welcome." He pulled her close against him. "Now, go back to sleep and we'll go have breakfast at a reasonable hour."

"I like how you think, Mr. Landry."

"I'm just being selfish because I like holding you close. You're one sexy lady, Brooke Harper."

She wrapped her arm over his waist. "You are the first man who ever made me feel that way."

Good, he liked sharing firsts with her. He also wished she would be here longer so he could do that all the time. "They're all blind and dumb."

"Can I tell you a secret?"

"Sure."

"When you're wearing those leather chaps with the fringe and your big belt buckle and cowboy hat, you're hard to resist."

He loved that he excited her. "If you want I can put on that gear for you. Us cowboys aim to please."

He acted as if he was getting out of bed and she reached to stop him. She was laughing. "I think my memory is pretty good. You can model for me later."

"My pleasure, ma'am." He leaned down and captured her mouth as he pulled her under him. What a way to start the day. He could get used to this.

LATER THAT MORNING, they'd left the B&B Diner in town stuffed with the biggest breakfast ever. Instead of going back to the cabin, Trent stopped by his ranch to check on Red Baron. Brooke didn't mind spending time with this man, or his horses.

She walked into the cool barn with Trent and inhaled

the now familiar smells: the hay, horses, even the manure. None of them bothered her anymore. Trent went off to check on Red so she went to greet some of her friends. The old buckskin horse, Cassie, eagerly greeted her, and Brooke returned the attention. Next she stopped by Trent's chestnut gelding, Rango. He was as big and powerful as his owner, then in the next stall was her favorite, sweet Raven.

"Hey, girl." She rubbed the black mare's neck. "How you doing? You resting today, after the two-day workout?"

The horse blew out a noisy breath and Brooke smiled. She pressed her face against the horse's neck and felt tears well up behind her eyes. How could she get attached to this animal, and so quickly? "I'm gonna miss you, girl," she murmured into the horse's soft coat, then released her.

She headed down the aisle when Trent came out of Red's stall. He looked at her and frowned. "What's wrong?"

She shook her head. "Nothing really, just saying goodbye to some friends."

Trent started to speak, but Brooke stopped him. "I don't want to talk about my staying or leaving. Nothing is going to change, Trent. So can't we just enjoy the time we have left?"

He nodded. "I was just about to say, why don't we go for a ride. There's plenty of amazing countryside you haven't seen yet."

She couldn't stop her excitement. "Really? Of course I want to go." She stopped. "Oh, wait. I promised Rory I'd look over the ranch's website and give him a brochure from the Dream Chaser Hotel."

"We can ride in the direction of the Bucking Q. This would be a good time to tell him he's your father."

Brooke glanced away. She knew Trent was right, but

she didn't want to spoil the tentative friendship that was starting between the two of them. "How do I start that conversation?"

AFTER A LEISURELY RIDE, but too soon for Brooke, they headed to the Bucking Q and her cabin. Trent kissed her, then gave her another pep talk on trusting Rory. She agreed, then stood there and watched the incredibly handsome man climb onto his horse. With the promise to meet her back here in a few hours, he rode off on Rango, leading Raven back to the Lucky Bar L.

With a last wave, Brooke watched the figures disappear over the rise. An ache circled in her chest and gripped her heart. She didn't want to leave this place, or Trent. Would it be possible to return here? To be a part of all this?

She pushed aside the fantasy and walked inside the cabin where she gathered the report and the hotel brochure from her laptop case and got into her car and went up to the main house.

As she parked at the back door and climbed out, she could feel her nerves starting to take over. Suddenly Laurel appeared on the steps and once again Brooke wondered how her sister would take the news.

There was a big grin on Laurel's face. "So how are you feeling today after you lassoed that cowboy last night?"

Brooke blushed. "What are you talking about?"

"Don't try and act innocent. I saw you and Trent making eyes at each other. Those looks got pretty heated at times, too." Laurel grew serious. "I know I've said this before—Trent is a good man, Brooke. And he seems to be pretty wrapped up in you. I've never seen him act this way with anyone. I hope you give him a chance."

That thrilled her. "I still have to go home."

"But you can come back here," her sister encouraged. "And I want to come and visit you in Las Vegas."

Hope spurred her. Maybe Rory would feel the same. "I'd like that very much."

Laurel hugged her tightly. "I'm so glad you came here, Brooke, and that you're my sister."

Brooke closed her eyes, working to hold back the emotions. "I'm glad you're my sister, too."

They pulled apart. "Sorry, I've got to go. I need to start a training session on a mistreated gelding. Can we get together later?"

"Sure, I'd like that. I need to see Rory. Is he around?"

Laurel nodded. "I just left him in the office. Go on in, it's the first room past the kitchen."

Brooke felt a little strange just walking in, but when she saw the kitchen was empty she felt better that Diane wasn't there. She hurried through the large room and into the hall, then continued looking for the elusive office. That was when she heard voices. She started to turn around, but when her name was mentioned, she couldn't. She went to the open door and saw Rory and Diane in a heated discussion.

"Diane, none of this is Brooke's fault."

Diane paced in front of the big desk. "That may or may not be true, but every time I see her, I'm reminded of that woman. Rory, she nearly destroyed us. I don't want Brooke here. Send her away."

Rory started to speak, but must have sensed her there and looked toward her and froze. "Brooke…"

Diane swung around and glared at her.

Brooke fumbled for the right words. "I'm sorry, Laurel told me to come in."

Diane didn't say a word, she just stormed out, leaving Rory and Brooke. There wasn't any choice now. Brooke's decision had been made. She released a calming breath and walked inside the room. "I'm sorry to interrupt, Rory."

"No, I must apologize that you had to hear that."

"Please, don't… I understand how your wife feels. I'm sorry my being here caused you both pain." Her throat tightened, and she held out her papers. "Here are the hotel brochures and some more information you might want to look at for ideas. I'm sorry I can't stay to look over your website with you, but I need to get on the road and home to my mother." She forced a smile, feeling her lips trembling. "Thank you so much for letting me stay here. I had such a great time. Good luck with the cabins."

His piercing gaze locked on hers. "I wish things could be different, Brooke."

She took one last look at her father, to memorize his face, trying to store away memories of him. She nodded. "Goodbye, Rory." She turned and walked slowly out of the house, then got in her car and made her way back to the cabin.

Once inside, she shut the door, and leaned against the wood frame, feeling her pounding heart. She had to leave here, and soon. She walked into the bedroom and began tossing her clothes into her bag, then straightened up the bed and bath. She hated the memories of time with Trent that flooded her head. She pushed them aside and carried her bag into the main room.

Then she took time to write Laurel a note, giving her a phone number and her Las Vegas address so she could stay in touch. Now, for the hardest part, composing the words to say goodbye to Trent. She decided to make it brief, believing he didn't want any more from her than what they'd shared this past week. Leaving the addressed envelopes on the counter, she looked around the cabin one last time. The pain in her chest made it difficult to breathe.

She closed her eyes, praying that she had the strength to move on. She wiped the tears from her face, then walked out and got into her car.

Sadness blanketed her as she drove under the Bucking Q Ranch sign. How did she let this place come to mean so much to her? She never meant to fall in love with Colorado. This life or this family…and Trent. But she couldn't have any of them.

TRENT RETURNED TO the Bucking Q and parked at the cabin. He was excited and had been a little apprehensive about leaving Brooke to show the report to Rory. Although he couldn't imagine his friend not accepting Brooke with open arms.

He parked in front of the cabins, surprised to see Brooke's car wasn't there. He opened the door and dread struck him as he went into the bedroom and found the closet emptied of Brooke's clothes.

Damn, she was gone. "No, she wouldn't leave without telling me." He went into the kitchen and found the note on the counter.

> *Trent,*
> *I'm sorry, something came up and I had to leave right away. I want to thank you for a wonderful time. Learning to ride Raven was incredible, and the roundup, too. Most of all it was the time I spent with you that was the best. I will never forget you.*
> *Brooke.*

Brooke was gone? What the hell happened? He rushed out of the cabin, jumped in his truck and drove to the house.

His tires squealed as he turned into the Quinns' driveway, then threw the gearshift into park and jumped out. He hurried through the back door, down the hall and into Rory's office. He saw his friend seated at the desk.

"Dammit, Rory! What did you say to make Brooke leave?"

Rory stood and came around the desk. "I didn't say anything. Brooke overheard Diane and me talking." He sighed. "Diane was upset."

"So you threw Brooke off the property because she brought back bad memories of Coralee. That's just great."

"Look, I didn't see any choice. Laurel and Brooke can still have a relationship."

"You have to know that Brooke had nothing to do with Coralee's behavior, but she's the one being punished." Trent threw up his arms. "Well, guess what? She's gone. Problem solved." He glared at Rory. "But it's not. Not by a long shot." He pointed to the manila envelope. "Did you even read the PI report?"

Rory shook his head. "That's only something Brooke brought me for our website."

"No, it's a PI report from Cody. He sent it to me the other night..." The night he'd made love to Brooke. The night she'd slept in his arms. He shook away the memory. "I showed it to Brooke and she promised to bring the information to you today."

Rory tore open the envelope. He scanned the page. "I'm not seeing anything..." His voice died out as his eyes widened, and he glanced at Trent. "She's the same age as Laurel. How is that possible?"

Trent nodded. "Because they're twins."

"Brooke's my daughter," he breathed and sank down into the chair. "Coralee kept her from me?"

"It seems so. Brooke didn't know about you until her mother's Alzheimer's had progressed and she began calling Brooke Laurel."

"How do you know all this?" Rory asked.

"She told me the other night, but I wanted Brooke to be the one to tell you."

"Oh, God." Tears formed in Rory's eyes. "Why? How did this happen?" He looked at Trent. "I swear I didn't know."

Trent shook his head. "Of course you didn't. It was Coralee who wasn't honest."

"You're right. But why did Brooke make up the story about being Laurel's half sister?"

Trent frowned. "She told me she only wanted to get Laurel to come to Las Vegas to see Coralee. She wasn't in the market for a father. I think her real reason was because she was afraid of getting rejected."

"And that's exactly what I did."

Laurel walked into the room. "Hey, Dad. Could you help…" She stopped after seeing Rory's sad expression. Was he ill? "What's wrong?"

Rory shook his head, then glanced at Trent.

"Tell her, she deserves to know," Trent said.

Okay, now she was panicked. "Somebody better tell me."

Rory looked at his daughter. "Seems that Brooke isn't your half sister—she's your twin sister."

A big smile spread across Laurel's face. "Really? Oh, wow! I can't believe it, I have a twin. How?" This was even better than she'd thought. She knew there was something special between them, more than the bond of half sisters. They'd shared a womb. She couldn't lose her now.

Rory explained everything to his daughter. She beamed and looked around. "Where is Brooke? I want to see her."

Trent delivered the bad news as he handed her the note that Brooke left for her. "She's on her way back to Las Vegas."

Rory took over. "I had no idea she was my daughter."

Another squeal came from Laurel when she realized Brooke had more of a connection to this family. "Oh, that's right, you're her dad, too. With Coralee sick, she needs someone to help her."

Rory glanced away. "I'm sorry, Laurel. I messed this up badly. I sent her away."

Laurel knew that, but she was aware that both her parents felt threatened. She only hoped that Brooke could understand that. "Well, then, you're just going to have to fix it because I'm not losing my sister."

TRENT ARRIVED BACK at his house and slammed the door in frustration. He'd called Brooke's cell phone, but it had gone straight to voice mail, and he didn't leave a message. What would he say? *Come back? I want a life with you?*

He cursed and was met with silence. The place was so cold and empty. He could still remember years ago when these rooms had been filled with laughter, happy Christmases and birthdays celebrated right here in this living room. It had all disappeared in one tragic day. Then about a year later, his mother had left, taking him away from everything he loved on the ranch, including his father... and any memories of Christopher. What made him think he could come back and change the past?

He shook away his morbid thoughts and walked upstairs, stripping off his shirt before heading to the shower. In his room, he paused when he saw the bed where he'd made love to Brooke that first time. His chest tightened. The sheets probably still smelled like her.

He walked to the window and looked out at the barn and corral. He'd worked hard to rebuild this place. For whom? Chris was gone, so was his father. His mother wouldn't set foot on the ranch. She'd made a new life for herself outside Denver, with a new husband and new sons.

His thoughts turned back to Brooke once again.

Why did she have to come here, into his home, leaving him more memories to bury? Now, she was gone, too. How was he supposed to get things back to normal and to stop thinking about her?

He walked to the dresser and pulled out clean underwear. His attention went to the stack of his father's unread letters.

You need to read them, Trent, Brooke had said. *Your father loved you.*

He picked up the stack of mail, released the string and began to sort through to find Wade Landry's last letter to his son. Trent checked the postmark. It was dated a week before his dad's death. Tears formed in his eyes as he opened the folded paper and began to read.

Dear son,

I got some time so I thought I'd write you and give you some news from back home. We had spring roundup this past weekend. Rory and Laurel helped, along with our crew of guys to bring the herd down from the high pasture. I only managed to ride half the day, before I wore out. I guess your old man isn't as young as he used to be.

My hope is one day when you retire from being a soldier, you'll come home and take over running the Lucky Bar L. It's a nice piece of grazing land, surrounded by the Rocky Mountains, a pretty view in any direction. There are also good neighbors on

*either side of the property. Rory would love to have
you nearby, too.*

*I know we haven't been close for a long time, and
I'm going to take the blame for most of that. After
Chris died, I closed up, shutting out you and your
mother. She didn't want to leave me. I pushed her
away until she had no choice but to go. I pushed
you away, too. You didn't deserve that, son. My only
excuse is that I was so filled with guilt about Chris
that it was hard to look you in the eye. No more.*

*For years I've left too many things unsaid, and
it's time to let you know the truth. I know you've always felt guilty about not taking Chris along with
you that day. I want you to stop blaming yourself.
I'm the reason Chris is dead.*

*When your brother got up that morning, he was
hurt that you left him behind. I told him if he wanted
to go along, then go after you. Chris was an experienced rider, and I had no doubt that he could find
you. I was wrong, dead wrong. It cost me my son,
and you your brother. I'm so sorry.*

*Now, I'm asking your forgiveness for all the
years I wasn't the father you needed. Please, don't
stay away from the ranch because of me. I won't be
around much longer. I've reconciled with the Lord,
and your mother. I need to tell you that I loved Chris
and you more than life.*

*I'm so proud of you, Trent. I just hope you can
find it in your heart to forgive me. But mostly, I don't
want you to have any regrets. Chris wouldn't want
you to spend any more time grieving him. He loved
you and would want you to live your life to the full-
est. That's what I want for you, too. Come home to
the Lucky Bar L, and make a good life.*

Goodbye, son.
Love,
Your father

Trent put down the letter as a rush of tears filled his eyes until the dam burst. He cried for the brother he'd lost, for the dad who had to carry this burden all these years, and for himself because he missed them all.

He didn't know how much time had passed, but he finally realized his dad was right. He needed to bury this for once and for all. He needed a new beginning.

What he needed was Brooke.

Chapter Seventeen

"Mother, you need to calm down, or you'll have to go back to your room," Brooke said as she sat on the sofa in the living room at the care facility.

Coralee Loretta Harper had a look of defiance across her once flawless face. Now her skin was lined by years of drinking and hard living. Although her beauty had faded, she was still slender and graceful.

Her mother turned her blue gaze toward her daughter. "You can't make me."

Brooke folded her arms. Her mother was lucid today, but very agitated, and demanding to get her way. Some things never changed. "Try me."

Coralee glared, but finally sat down on the sofa. "You promised me, Brooke. You were going to bring Laurel here for me."

Only back from Colorado two days, Brooke had to go to work at the casino right away. It seemed that she'd have her dealer's job for a while. The manager's position at Dream Chaser Hotel that she'd been offered was for their Reno, Nevada, location. She had to turn it down. So she wasn't in the best mood today.

"I told you already, not everyone can stop their lives to do what you want."

But Brooke always had. She was at the top of that list

for enabling her mother, or she would have never gone to Colorado. She felt a rush of happiness, knowing she was glad she had gone to Hidden Springs. She met her sister, her father and her first lover, even if their time together had been so short.

She'd tried not to think about Trent, but gave up. She'd relived their week together over and over again during her drive back. Even though he couldn't offer her a future, she had no regrets about loving the man.

Her mother's voice broke through her reverie. "Did Laurel at least say when she was coming to see me?"

It had surprised Brooke that she hadn't heard from Laurel. Maybe her sister was upset because she hadn't told her the entire truth. And what about Rory? Wouldn't he at least acknowledge that Brooke was his daughter, or had Diane prevented him from contacting her?

"Well, I want you to call her, and tell her to come," her mother demanded.

The pretty redheaded director, Erin, walked into the public room that was shared by the four residents at Carlton Care Facility. Up until three months ago, that had included Erin's disabled husband, Jarred. The ex-marine had been severely wounded in Afghanistan. He'd died due to complications from his injuries. Brooke had only met Jarred once while she'd worked here some weekends. She wondered how Erin had dealt with the loss.

"Maybe she'll come visit you tomorrow, Coralee," Erin said. "Now, it's time for you to go to bed."

Coralee pouted. "It's still early."

Erin was persistent. She had to be, dealing with Alzheimer's patients. "Once you get bathed and into your gown, it will be bedtime."

Coralee finally relented. She stood and walked away with Carol, the second shift nurse.

"Put on the blue gown," Brooke called to her. "The color makes your eyes shine."

That got her a smile from her mother. "It's my favorite, too." Coralee's whole mood changed as she left the room.

Brooke collapsed on the sofa and Erin joined her. "I didn't realize there would be such a change in her in just a week."

"She actually did very well while you were gone." Erin looked her in the eyes. "She just knows how to push your buttons."

Brooke knew that was true. "I've let her have her way for so long, I don't know how to stop."

"At this stage of her disease, it would be impossible for Coralee to change." Erin reached across and covered Brooke's hand. "Let's talk about you now. Tell me about your sister and your father."

Brooke forced a smile. "Laurel is wonderful, but I'm not sure she'll come to see Coralee. We talked about it some, but then I had to leave suddenly."

Over the years growing up, Brooke hadn't had many friends. That had changed when she met Erin. Over the past six months they'd shared a lot. She'd told Erin about all the wonderful things she got to do while in Colorado, then how it all fell apart.

"None of them have called me," Brooke said. "Not that I blame them. I wasn't exactly truthful when I first arrived." She was hoping Trent would contact her. "Trent never made me any promises, either."

"That doesn't mean he shouldn't have called you," Erin said, shaking her head. "At least to see if you made it home."

"I turned off my phone. I can't expect them to drop everything. Trent even told me from the beginning that he didn't do commitments."

Erin gripped Brooke's hand. "That seems to be a typical guy's line."

She put on a smile. "It still was the best week of my life. I met my sister and father." She hated how much she hurt leaving them. Aching to be a part of a family. Guess that wasn't in the picture for her. She stood. "I'd better go and say good-night to Coralee, then I need to head home and get some sleep."

Erin stood and hugged her. "If you need me, I'm here for you."

At the sound of the doorbell, they broke apart. "Who could that be this late?" Erin and Brooke went to the door and checked the security camera. On the porch were Laurel and Rory.

Brooke gasped. "Oh, no. It's my sister, Laurel, and Rory."

Erin smiled. "Should I send them away?"

"No! I just don't know what to say to them."

"Try hello," Erin said, then released the lock on the door and opened it. "Welcome to Carlton Care Facility, I'm Erin Carlton."

Laurel spoke first. "Nice to meet you, Mrs. Carlton. I'm Laurel Quinn, Brooke Harper's sister."

Rory stepped in behind her, holding his cowboy hat in his hand. With a nod, he said, "Mrs. Carlton. I'm Rory Quinn, Brooke's father. We were wondering if we could speak with her."

Erin motioned with her hand. "Yes, she is here."

At the mention of her name, Brooke released a breath, trying to relax. *Stay calm*, she told herself, then stepped into the entry. "Hello, Rory and Laurel."

Laurel smiled. "Hi, Brooke."

Erin spoke up. "Why don't we all go into the other

room and get more comfortable, and you can talk with her?"

Brooke led the way and they followed her into the living room, but no one sat down. She had no idea what to say to them, but since they were here, she felt hopeful.

Laurel spoke first. "I should start, Brooke. I'm sorry you felt you had to leave. It's not what I wanted at all." She glanced at her father. "I probably didn't tell you how happy I was that you're my sister, but now knowing that you're my twin—" she shook her head "—I feel even closer to you."

Brooke nodded. "I'm sorry I didn't tell you right away. I'd planned to, but you had gone to Denver…" She stole a quick glance at Rory. "I couldn't just blurt it out."

Rory stepped forward. "And I didn't help matters by blaming you for everything your mother had done."

She shook her head. "No, it's okay. You have to protect your family. I understand that."

Rory nervously toyed with his cowboy hat. "But you are my family, Brooke. Just as much as Laurel is mine."

Her heart skipped a couple of beats. A flood of emotion filled her and spilled out in tears. "I'm still a stranger to you."

"I don't want us to be strangers, Brooke. I know you're an adult, but if there's any space in your life for me, I'd like to get to know you."

"Really?" She glanced back at Laurel. "I don't want to intrude in your lives. I mean, Diane doesn't need me to disrupt her family."

"Mom is the one who arranged our flights to come here today. She also sends her apologies for not being fair to you. She knows now that she shouldn't have blamed you for what Coralee had done."

Rory took over. "Diane wanted us to be sure to let you know that you're welcome at our ranch and in our family."

Brooke's hand covered her mouth, but she couldn't stop the tears.

"I'm so sorry, Brooke," Rory said. "If you'll give me another chance, I'll try and do better."

She nodded. "I'd like that."

Rory smiled and pulled Brooke into a tight embrace. "I want you to be part of our family, Brooke," he whispered. "Will you be my daughter?"

Brooke sobbed and held on to the big man. She'd always been afraid to dream of a family, because she didn't want to be disappointed. She wiped away her tears and looked at him. "I always wanted a…dad."

Rory kissed her check. "Well, you got me for keeps."

Laurel came and hugged her, too. "You're even more than my sister, you're my twin." She hugged her tighter. "I can't wait for you to come back to the ranch."

Brooke raised a hand. "I can't come back for a while, Laurel. I mean, Coralee is here. I also have my job." She had to take care of her mother.

"Speaking of Coralee, if it's not too late now," Laurel said, "I guess it's time I met our mother."

Around ten o'clock that evening Trent looked around the not-so-ideal neighborhood. It was run-down, and graffiti decorated a lot of the block walls. He'd parked his rental car at the curb in front of Brooke's apartment complex. It was hard to believe that she lived here.

What kind of childhood had she had growing up in a place like this? A lot worse than he could imagine. Well, he didn't want her staying here any longer than necessary. She needed to go back to Colorado with him, but that might take some convincing.

He checked his phone and found a text from Laurel saying they'd talked with Brooke at the care facility. Everything had gone well. Trent had dropped them off earlier to see Brooke and Coralee. They were going to take a cab back to the hotel. Now it was Trent's turn to convince Brooke that he wanted her in his life.

Brooke's familiar compact pulled in and parked under the streetlight, then she got out of the car. Hoping not to startle her, he called her name as he got out of his car and immediately identified himself.

She swung around, looking shocked. "Trent?"

He walked toward her, fighting the urge to take her in his arms. "Hi, babe."

She tensed. "What are you doing here?"

He didn't blame her for being suspicious. "I need to see you. Why did you leave without talking to me?"

She shrugged. "Rory didn't want me there, so I thought it best I leave. I left you a note."

"I got it, but I thought we were closer than that."

"Closer than what, Trent? You said you didn't do relationships. Besides if you were so upset, why didn't you call me?"

"I did call, but I couldn't leave a message. I had a lot of things to deal with first before I showed up at your door." He glanced around the area. "Could we talk inside?"

She hesitated, then nodded. Together they walked past several apartment doors. Some had children's toys scattered around the yard and others, overflowing trashcans. He could hear loud voices coming from some of the units. Not a place he wanted her staying in. Finally they came to hers and she unlocked the door, then flicked on the lights and walked in.

He glanced around the tiny room with a small kitchenette. The furniture was worn and out of date, including the small box television that sat on a table. The one thing he did notice was that the place was immaculately clean.

Brooke tossed her keys on the table and set her purse down. She gave him a defiant look as if challenging him to say something. "Home sweet home. This is how I live, Trent."

She wasn't happy to see him and he couldn't blame her. Ignoring her comment, he walked across the room and cupped her face in his hands and kissed her. Long and hard, then easing into a slow devouring of that sweet mouth of hers, so eager for her familiar taste. Finally he let her go. "God, I've missed you."

She fell back a step, then she composed herself. "Well, you shouldn't have come here. Your life is in Colorado and mine is here." She glanced at him. "I won't ever forget the week we had together, but you were right. There's no future for us. I don't want you to think that I expect anything when I come to visit Rory and Laurel."

He was thrilled that her father and sister had worked things out. But he wasn't going to let this woman push him away. "Oh, I expect a lot, Brooke. I'm going to expect to spend time with you. You're not getting rid of me."

She blinked those big green eyes. "But I thought…"

He took her hand and sat her down on the sofa, then seated himself next to her, never letting go of her hand.

"First of all," he began. "I was wrong about a lot of things, and that includes needing anyone in my life." His gaze met hers. "You made me see a lot of things, Brooke. And my father's letter helped show me that, too."

"Oh, Trent, you read them?"

"Only the last one he wrote to me," Trent confessed. "But I'm planning on reading the rest of them soon." He released a breath. "Yesterday I saddled Rango and rode out to the ravine…where Chris died." He felt the emotion clogging his throat, but he pushed through it. "I've avoided the place for years, but yesterday in the early-morning sunlight, I found peace and even felt close to him. It's the first time in a very long time."

He looked at Brooke and saw the smile he'd come to love. "I'm so happy for you, Trent."

He squeezed her hand. "I still have a ways to go, but I don't want to do it alone. You made me realize how empty my life has been. All the years I've avoided any connection to people, even with the Quinns."

She started to speak, but he placed his finger over her lips. "Let me finish, before I lose my nerve."

She nodded.

"That first night we made love, you gave me a precious gift. I never felt like that before with another woman, but I was still afraid to let you in. The last thing I wanted was for you to be stuck with a man who carried guilt with him. My dad's letter made me see that we all took the blame for Chris's death. And in truth, it was a tragic accident."

His gaze locked on hers. "I know that now, Brooke. You tried to tell me, but I didn't want to listen. I'm sorry I pushed you away."

Brooke shook with emotion as she reached up and touched Trent's handsome face. "I understand, Trent. I'm just happy you're here now."

He smiled and her heart melted. "So you're glad to see me."

She wasn't afraid to say it. "More than you know."

"Good, because this guy is crazy in love with you and I want a life with you."

She gasped as her eyes searched his face. "Oh, Trent."

"I know it's only been a little over a week, but I love you."

She couldn't stop her words, either. "I love you, too."

His mouth covered hers in a hungry kiss. When he released her, they were both breathless. She quickly came down from her high remembering there were other problems. "I can't go back to Colorado with you. My mother…"

He shook his head. "Us being apart isn't an option. If being here is best for your mother, then I'll move here, or we'll move back to the ranch and find a specialized facility for Coralee close by."

"Oh, Trent, you can't give up the Lucky Bar L."

"You think I'm going to give you up?" He shook his head. "Never." He kissed her again. "We'll figure this out. Together."

She loved the idea, but she had Rory and Laurel to consider. "You make it sound so easy."

"It's true. None of us know how long your mother will be able to remember you and Laurel, but you have that time now, and I wouldn't take that away from you. I know how important family is, and how quickly they can be torn from you."

She could only nod as tears took over. This was the sweetest man. Trent lifted her into his arms and held her close and she felt her burden ease. She'd never had anyone to depend on before.

"I didn't mean to make you cry. I want to help you. I know your mother is far from perfect, but she's your mother, and of course you love her. We're going to find a way to take care of her."

She raised her head from his chest. "Thank you. I'm so glad you came into my life."

He swallowed hard. "No, Brooke, I need to thank you for taking on a stubborn ex–sergeant major." He paused and cupped her face. "Brooke Harper, I know we haven't known each other long, but I love you with all my heart, and I want to spend the rest of my life with you." He reached inside his jacket pocket and pulled out a small box. He managed to flip it open with one hand to expose a ring. "Will you marry me?"

Brooke stared down at the pear-shaped diamond sparkling up at her.

"Oh, Trent," she gasped.

"I hope you like it."

"I've never seen anything so beautiful."

His eyes met hers. "I have. *You* are more beautiful. That first day you came to the ranch, I couldn't keep my eyes off you."

"But I looked like Laurel. How come you were never attracted to her?"

He frowned. "Please, she's like a sister and just as annoying." He sobered. "I love you, Brooke. I want you as my wife. Say yes."

She pushed aside her doubts, trusting this man to be there for her. "Oh, yes, I'll marry you."

His mouth closed over hers in a kiss that convinced Brooke that with this man, anything was possible.

Trent tore his mouth away. "Please tell me that doorway leads to a bedroom."

She nodded. "My bed is small."

He stood up with her in his arms. "Not a problem, I plan on staying pretty close to you."

THE NEXT MORNING, Brooke awoke with Trent asleep next to her. He greeted her with a kiss, letting her know he couldn't get enough of her, and they made love again.

Finally they got out of bed and showered together. She loved sharing so many firsts with Trent. Running late, they dressed in a hurry and drove to the hotel to have breakfast with Rory and Laurel.

They both were greeted with hugs and sat down to

coffee. Rory was the one who glanced back and forth between the two. Brooke felt a blush warm her cheeks.

"Is there something you need to tell me, son?" Rory asked.

Trent put her arm around Brooke and brought her close. "Yes, there is. I asked Brooke to marry me last night and she said yes."

Laurel squealed and jumped up to hug her sister. "I'm so happy for you." Then she gave her a pouty look. "I guess there won't be any girls' nights or sleepovers, huh?"

"You got that right. I'm not letting Brooke out of my sight."

"She'll be close at least," Laurel said.

Rory took his turn to hug Brooke. "I just found you to lose you to this guy. I'd argue it was too soon, but you picked the best man."

"I think so, too."

They all sat down to breakfast and talked wedding plans. It was starting out to be the best day ever.

AN HOUR LATER, they drove to Carlton Care Facility to see Coralee.

Brooke led the way inside, then went into the public room. There was Erin seated with Coralee. It had been too late last night for the Quinns to see her mother, and Brooke wasn't sure if today would be any better. Would this visit be too much of a shock to her?

"Hello, Mother," Brooke said.

Slowly, her mother looked up at her, then her attention went to Laurel.

Her expression changed and finally she smiled, but with tears in her eyes. "Oh, Laurel, you came back."

Coralee stood as Laurel crossed the room and took

their mother's hands. Brooke was so grateful to see how her sister handled the situation.

"Hello, Mother," Laurel began, her voice trembling. "It's been a long time. I've missed you."

Coralee's hand was shaking as she touched Laurel's face. "You are so beautiful. I knew you would be."

"Thank you. I've been told I look like my mother."

Coralee blushed. "I've been told I was beautiful by a lot of men." She looked at Brooke who realized she was looking past her. Brooke glanced in the direction of her mother's attention. Rory. She wandered over to him, her gaze searching his face. "Do I know you?"

Rory smiled. "It's been a long time, Coralee. But I heard you sing one night a long time ago."

Trent stood back with Brooke and watched as both Rory and Laurel talked with Coralee. They were kind and gentle, even though this woman had kept their daughter and sister away from them. Now sadly, Coralee's memory was slowly fading.

Trent hugged Brooke closer. She'd missed too many things in her life, and from this day on, he was going to let her know how much she was loved.

Brooke looked up at him, tears in her eyes. "Thank you for being here. This is making Mother so happy. I just hope she can remember it for a while."

He leaned down and kissed her. "You will remember, and that's what is important. And also remember that I love you, Brooke."

He pulled his future wife closer. He wanted to make sure that she knew he was there for her. She wasn't alone anymore. They were family now.

Epilogue

Over the past two months, Brooke's life had changed drastically, and all for the good. No, for the wonderful.

She'd resigned from her long-time job at the casino, and given notice at her apartment complex. She packed only her clothes and a few special items. All the rest of her second-hand furniture, she'd given away.

The most difficult thing about leaving the city was transferring her mother out of the Carlton Care Facility. It was hard to leave Erin, but from what her friend had told her, she needed to make some changes in her life, too. Maybe even relocate. Would she come to Colorado, as well?

Luckily, they found her mother a wonderful place in Hidden Springs that specialized in Alzheimer's patients. Along with Trent, Brooke drove Coralee to Colorado and moved her into a new home with great views of the Rocky Mountains. So far, Coralee seemed happy there.

Riding across the open range, Brooke slowed and pulled back on her reins to slow Raven. This was one of her new favorite things to do since moving here. Riding horseback across the grassy valley dotted with cattle, she couldn't stop the rush of emotions. Who would have thought six months ago that now she would be married to a cowboy and living on a ranch in Colorado?

She glanced down at her wedding rings. Deciding they didn't want to wait, she and Trent had been married in Las Vegas with Laurel, Rory, Erin and her mother present. Nothing fancy, except Laurel convinced her to buy a new dress for the occasion.

So they'd gone shopping and Brooke found a satin and lace mid-length dress at one of the many outlet stores in the area. Trent had worn a Western-cut tux jacket with black jeans. Rory looked sharp, too, as he walked her down the aisle. It was a perfect day to marry the perfect man.

Now nearly two months later, Brooke burrowed deeper into her new heavier jacket Trent had bought her, along with new boots and cowboy hat. She loved her new life on the ranch.

She patted Raven's neck, loving the time she got to ride the sweet mare. With winter coming, she didn't know how long she could continue to be on horseback.

She heard her name and looked over her shoulder to see Trent riding toward her. She felt that familiar jolt in her chest and warmth surrounded her heart, as it always did whenever her man was close.

Trent pulled up on Rango's reins. "You're getting too fast for me, I can't keep up." He leaned forward and kissed her. "What's your hurry?"

"No hurry. I just love the freedom of riding fast. And like you said, snow will be coming soon, and I won't be able to ride for a while. How did the final inspection go on the cabins?"

"Great, they signed off on everything. We're ready to rent. We've already booked a company Christmas party. And I've been hired as the outfitter for a hunting party in two weeks. All this thanks to your new website."

"Me? I just gave a few suggestions on where you and Rory should advertise."

"Well, it helped. Thank you."

"Hey, I need to pull my weight around here. I'm not working."

He frowned. "Is that what you think, that you aren't working?"

She shrugged. "I've worked since I started a paper route when I was twelve. It's strange to me."

"You take care of the website, and you help decorate the cabins, and then there are the daily trips into town to visit your mother. You have plenty to keep you busy. Unless you want a job."

"Don't we need my income, especially with my mother's extra care?"

Trent shifted his horse closer and leaned down and kissed his wife. "No, we don't need your income. Remind me when we get home to show you the finances, including the deed to the Lucky Bar L. Now as my wife, you are part owner, too."

"You don't need to do that, Trent."

He knew that Brooke had grown up with nothing. He wanted her to know that she'd always have a home. "What is mine is yours."

"You have a lot more than I do."

"All I want is you." Trent couldn't help grinning at his bride. "I'm having Ricky and Mike bring the herd down from the high range tomorrow. I don't want to lose any of the new calves with this storm coming."

"Could I ride out, too?"

"I thought you and Laurel were going to visit Coralee in the morning, and then bake pies for Thanksgiving. In case you want to know, pecan is my favorite."

She laughed. "I think you've mentioned it a few times."

He couldn't stop staring at her. She was so beautiful, and he wanted her even more. "Have I told you lately how much I love you?"

Her gaze softened. "Yes, you have, but I'll never get tired of hearing you say those words."

"I have an idea. Why don't we race back to the ranch and I'll show you?"

She giggled. "I like the way you think, Mr. Landry." She kicked her heels into Raven's sides and took off. Trent was right there beside her.

THANKSGIVING DAY WAS cold and cloudy with the promise of a big snowstorm by nightfall. That excited Brooke, but not as much as the news she couldn't wait to share with Trent.

She'd dressed in gray wool slacks and a cream-colored sweater and black leather boots. This was her first holiday dinner with the Quinns, her family. And her news made it an extra special day. After a last check in the mirror, she went downstairs to find Trent. The pies and salad were packed up and ready for the trip to the Bucking Q Ranch. This was the first Thanksgiving she'd ever truly felt blessed.

She walked into the kitchen and found her husband drinking a cup of coffee at the table. Usually she got his undivided attention the first thing in the morning, but today they had to get moving fast with chores.

Trent smiled at her. "You look mighty pretty."

"Thank you." She kissed him, but when she started to pull away, he held on tight.

"Maybe we should head back to bed. I'm sure the Quinns will understand if we show up late."

She laughed nervously. "I like your thinking, but could we talk first?"

He sobered. "Sure, babe. What's the problem?"

Brooke sank down in the chair, her knees a little weak. "It's not a problem exactly, just not planned." Her gaze met his beautiful brown eyes. Would their child have them? "I'm pregnant."

"Whoa." He straightened, then a big grin spread across his face. "I thought we were careful." He shook his head and picked her up, swinging her around in a circle. "Oh, my God. We're having a baby."

Brooke laughed and he finally put her down. "So I take it you like the idea?" she asked.

He cupped her face and kissed her tenderly. "I love the idea. I already love him or her. And I love you so much." There were tears in his eyes as he touched her stomach. "Lucky us. We have each other, and now a baby."

"I feel the same way. Lucky us."

He held her close and Brooke never knew life could be this wonderful. She'd been blessed with the family she'd always wanted, always dreamed of.

AFTER A VISIT with Coralee, Trent drove Brooke to the Bucking Q for Thanksgiving dinner. Since moving here, Brooke and Diane had managed to become polite friends, and that was fine with Brooke. This woman had a lot to deal with, especially with Coralee moving so close to her home.

Diane and Laurel would always be mother and daughter. Nothing would change that. So Brooke tried to stay in the background. But now with the baby coming, she hoped that Diane would play a bigger part in their lives. Brooke hoped to encourage her to be a grandma to her baby.

"We're here," Trent called from the kitchen doorway.

Smiling, Diane waved them inside. "Well, come on in."

So many aromas teased Brooke's nose as Trent carried

their box of pies. He didn't want her handling anything heavy. Okay, she loved that he was spoiling her. She was glad there was only the immediate family coming today. This was her first holiday and she wanted to be with her father and sister and husband. She touched her stomach, and their baby. She was excited and terrified at the same time. Was she ready to be a mother?

She felt Trent's arm come around her back and pull her close. She looked up and he brushed a kiss on her mouth. How did she get so lucky to find him? This baby was lucky, too.

He nuzzled her cheek and whispered, "We don't have to tell anyone yet. We can keep it to ourselves for a little longer."

She nodded. "Sounds like a good idea."

Rory walked into the room with a big smile and hugged her. It still took Brooke aback whenever the man showed her affection. She hugged him back. "How is Coralee today?" he asked.

Brooke knew this situation was difficult. "She's doing fine. She wasn't very talkative this morning, but that's to be expected with the progression of the disease."

Diane stepped in. "I can wrap up some leftovers so you and Laurel can take them to her later."

Brooke was touched. "Thank you, Diane. That would be nice." She looked around. "Where is Laurel, anyway?"

"Where do you think?" Diane said. "With her horses."

Just then the back door opened, then slammed and Laurel walked in. She threw up her hands. "You're never going to believe who came home." She jammed her hands on her hips. "Just guess. I mean, just take a wild guess?"

Brooke opened her mouth, but closed it. "I have no idea."

"You wouldn't know about him, anyway. Lucky you."

She turned to her parents. "Kase Rawlins is back in town. Could my life get any worse?" She stormed out of the kitchen.

Brooke had a feeling things were going to get really interesting. She glanced at her husband and he was grinning. She couldn't wait to meet this Kase Rawlins.

* * * * *

COMING NEXT MONTH FROM

⊞ HARLEQUIN®

American Romance®

Available April 5, 2016

#1589 TEXAS REBELS: JUDE
Texas Rebels • by Linda Warren
When Paige Wheeler returns to the small Texas town where she grew up, will Jude Rebel be able to tell her he kept the child she gave up for adoption...or will he continue to protect his heart?

#1590 FALLING FOR THE RANCHER
Cupid's Bow, Texas • by Tanya Michaels
Rancher Jarrett Ross is a man who blames himself for putting his sister in a wheelchair. Hiring physical therapist Sierra Bailey means Sierra's off-limits—no matter how much he wants her.

#1591 A COWBOY'S CLAIM
Cowboys of the Rio Grande • by Marin Thomas
When rodeo cowboy Victor Vicario is given temporary custody of his nephew, he asks barrel racer Tanya McGee for help. Victor knows it can't last, but their little family *feels* real...

#1592 THE ACCIDENTAL COWBOY
Angel Crossing, Arizona • by Heidi Hormel
When former bronc rider Lavonda Leigh agrees to guide an archaeologist through rough ranch terrain, she's not expecting a smoldering Scottish cowboy! Jones Kincaid is sure to dig up trouble in Arizona...

YOU CAN FIND MORE INFORMATION ON UPCOMING HARLEQUIN® TITLES, FREE EXCERPTS AND MORE AT WWW.HARLEQUIN.COM.

HARCNM0316

REQUEST YOUR FREE BOOKS!
2 FREE NOVELS PLUS 2 FREE GIFTS!

 HARLEQUIN®

~American ~Romance®

LOVE, HOME & HAPPINESS

YES! Please send me 2 FREE Harlequin® American Romance® novels and my 2 FREE gifts (gifts are worth about $10). After receiving them, if I don't wish to receive any more books, I can return the shipping statement marked "cancel." If I don't cancel, I will receive 4 brand-new novels every month and be billed just $4.74 per book in the U.S. or $5.49 per book in Canada. That's a savings of at least 12% off the cover price! It's quite a bargain! Shipping and handling is just 50¢ per book in the U.S. and 75¢ per book in Canada.* I understand that accepting the 2 free books and gifts places me under no obligation to buy anything. I can always return a shipment and cancel at any time. Even if I never buy another book, the two free books and gifts are mine to keep forever.

154/354 HDN GHZZ

Name	(PLEASE PRINT)

Address	Apt. #

City	State/Prov.	Zip/Postal Code

Signature (if under 18, a parent or guardian must sign)

Mail to the **Reader Service:**
IN U.S.A.: P.O. Box 1867, Buffalo, NY 14240-1867
IN CANADA: P.O. Box 609, Fort Erie, Ontario L2A 5X3

Want to try two free books from another line?
Call 1-800-873-8635 or visit www.ReaderService.com.

* Terms and prices subject to change without notice. Prices do not include applicable taxes. Sales tax applicable in N.Y. Canadian residents will be charged applicable taxes. Offer not valid in Quebec. This offer is limited to one order per household. Not valid for current subscribers to Harlequin American Romance books. All orders subject to credit approval. Credit or debit balances in a customer's account(s) may be offset by any other outstanding balance owed by or to the customer. Please allow 4 to 6 weeks for delivery. Offer available while quantities last.

Your Privacy—The Reader Service is committed to protecting your privacy. Our Privacy Policy is available online at www.ReaderService.com or upon request from the Reader Service.

We make a portion of our mailing list available to reputable third parties that offer products we believe may interest you. If you prefer that we not exchange your name with third parties, or if you wish to clarify or modify your communication preferences, please visit us at www.ReaderService.com/consumerchoice or write to us at Reader Service Preference Service, P.O. Box 9062, Buffalo, NY 14240-9062. Include your complete name and address.

HAR15

SPECIAL EXCERPT FROM

◆ **HARLEQUIN**®
™

·American ·Romance®

*Jude Rebel and Paige Wheeler were teenage
sweethearts who had a baby together. A baby Paige
thought that they gave away. She doesn't know that
Jude went back for his son and has been raising
the boy alone. And now Paige is back in Horseshoe,
wondering what happened to their child…*

Read on for a sneak peek of
TEXAS REBELS: JUDE,
the fourth book in **Linda Warren**'s
***TEXAS REBELS** miniseries.*

Jude parked at the curb of the new Horseshoe Park and
made his way to where he saw Paige sitting at a picnic
table. The first thing he'd noticed was she was slimmer
and her hair was more blond than brown. It suited her.
Her face still held that same sweet innocence that had
first attracted him to her. But now there was a maturity
about her that was just as attractive.

She got up and ran to him, then wrapped her arms
around his waist and hugged him. He froze, which was
more the reaction of the boy he used to be. But the man in
him recognized all those old feelings that had bound him
to her years ago. Maybe some things just never changed.

When he didn't return the hug, she went back to
the table and he eased onto the bench across from her,
removing his hat. The wind rustled through the tall oaks
and he took a moment to gather his thoughts. It was like

gathering bits and pieces from his past to guide him. What should he say? What should he do?

"You look good," she said. "You filled out. The teenage boy I used to date doesn't seem to exist anymore."

"He grew up, and so have you. The young girl of long ago has matured into a beautiful woman."

"Thank you." She tilted her head slightly to smile at him and his heart raced like a wild mustang's at the look he remembered well. "You were always good for my ego."

He didn't shift or act nervous. He had to be the man he was supposed to be. For Zane. And for himself.

"How's California?"

"Great. I'm busy, so I don't get to see a lot of it. But I've enjoyed my stay there."

"I'm glad you had the chance to make your dream come true." He meant that with all his heart. But a small part of him wanted her to love him enough to have stayed and raised their son together. "Do you still work on the ranch?" she asked quickly, as if she wanted to change the subject.

"Yes. I'll always be a cowboy."

She fiddled with her hands in her lap. "I heard you have a son." Her eyes caught his, and all the guilt hit him, blindsiding him.

"Yes." *Our son. The one you gave away.*

Don't miss TEXAS REBELS: JUDE
by Linda Warren,
available April 2016 everywhere
Harlequin® American Romance®
books and ebooks are sold.

www.Harlequin.com

Copyright © 2016 by Linda Warren

HAREXP0316

Turn your love of reading into rewards you'll love with

Harlequin My Rewards

Join for FREE today at www.HarlequinMyRewards.com

Earn **FREE BOOKS** of your choice.

Experience **EXCLUSIVE OFFERS** and contests.

Enjoy **BOOK RECOMMENDATIONS** selected just for you.

PLUS! Sign up now and get **500** points right away!

Earn **FREE REWARDS**
HarlequinMyRewards.com
Join Today!

MYR16R

Love the Harlequin book you just read?

Your opinion matters.

Review this book on your favorite book site, review site, blog or your own social media properties and share your opinion with other readers!

Be sure to connect with us at:
Harlequin.com/Newsletters
Facebook.com/HarlequinBooks
Twitter.com/HarlequinBooks

HARLEQUIN®

A *Romance* FOR EVERY MOOD™

JUST CAN'T GET ENOUGH?

Join our social communities
and talk to us online.

You will have access to the latest
news on upcoming titles and special
promotions, but most importantly,
you can talk to other fans about your
favorite Harlequin reads.

Harlequin.com/Community

f Facebook.com/HarlequinBooks

t Twitter.com/HarlequinBooks

p Pinterest.com/HarlequinBooks

HSOCIAL

THE WORLD IS BETTER WITH

Romance

Harlequin has everything from contemporary, passionate and heartwarming to suspenseful and inspirational stories.

Whatever your mood, we have a romance just for you!

Connect with us to find your next great read, special offers and more.

f /HarlequinBooks

🐦 @HarlequinBooks

www.HarlequinBlog.com

www.Harlequin.com/Newsletters

 HARLEQUIN®

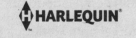 A *Romance* FOR EVERY MOOD™

www.Harlequin.com

SERIESHALOAD2015